THE UNDESIRABLE DUKE

CHRISTMAS IN LONDON (BOOK 2)

ROSE PEARSON

© Copyright 2024 by Rose Pearson - All rights reserved.

In no way is it legal to reproduce, duplicate, or transmit any part of this document by either electronic means or in printed format. Recording of this publication is strictly prohibited and any storage of this document is not allowed unless with written permission from the publisher. All rights reserved.

Respective author owns all copyrights not held by the publisher.

THE UNDESIRABLE DUKE

CHAPTER ONE

"What is this?" Samuel Fletcher, Duke of Yarmouth's hazel eyes flashed in anger as he held the recently opened letter up high for all to see, despite only a single male servant being present. "Speak," he ordered.

"I am not certain, Your Grace. It was a letter delivered from London."

The servant's voice was shaky, and he trembled in his boots as the Duke stared at him, his eyes narrowing.

"Thank you. Pardon me, it's not your fault that the letter is not what I wanted. You are dismissed."

With an absentminded gesture of his hand, he dismissed the servant who had delivered the letter to him. The servant left the room as fast as his legs were able to take him, and the door slammed behind him.

In Samuel's hand was a newspaper clipping of an article, the reckless words of which would certainly raise more than a few eyebrows. And it probably had already, he feared, as he continued to read. Someone was pitching the gammon, since not a single word in the article was accurate. The author, whoever it was, certainly did not have their facts straight. Samuel turned his attention to the letter which had enclosed the article, and immediately recognized his good friend's penmanship. His eyes darted across the page as he devoured the words on each line. His face tensed, his brow furrowing deeply, leaving creases on his skin.

"I do not believe this," he muttered, throwing the letter onto the desk before him.

"Whatever is the matter, Your Grace?"

While he read the letter, Samuel had completely forgotten his friend's presence, and now, after a momentary start, he exhaled slowly. He raked his fingers through his dark brown hair with pure agitation and stared at his friend, Lord Felmar. Despite Samuel's semi-hermit state in Cornwall, he and Lord Felmar were good friends. Hopefully, his friend would forgive his manner - it had been a long while since such fury had coursed through him, but this was both unacceptable and maddening. An unknown author had written an article in a London newspaper, claiming the most preposterous things about him.

Lies. All lies.

Who would believe such Canterbury tales? The residents of London, of course. They were starved for gossip and rumors during the Winter months, for, since the Season had come to a close, there was not much for the gossips to do.

Samuel had been residing at his country home for nearly two years, come this winter, and had not set foot outside Cornwall during that time. How on earth could such lies be taken as the truth? Of course, he was also well aware of how things operated in London. The rumor mills churned, regardless of what time of the year it was, but he had not expected to be involved in a rumor.

He turned his attention to a large portrait on the wall opposite him. His late father stared tight-jawed at him, as though he was already filled with disappointment at his only son.

"What an utter pack of lies!"

Lord Felmar appeared befuddled by Samuel's statement and tilted his head to the side.

"I beg your pardon, Your Grace?"

"It appears that someone, who is nameless at this point, is intentionally spreading scandals throughout London about me."

"I still do not follow."

Samuel handed the newspaper snippet to Lord Felmar, and after reading it, Felmar's brows shot up.

"Your Grace, what do you intend to do about this?"

"I am not quite certain," he said and chuckled. "At first, I was infuriated, understandably. But then, I became amused that someone would publish such things about me. The idea that I retreated to Cornwall because I had overextended myself is ludicrous. I have never enjoyed gambling, and I am far from financial ruin."

"And the claim of you frequently visiting undesirable haunts?"

Samuel glanced at Lord Felmar and raised his hands.

"I may be a man with desires, but certainly not these

kinds. I am not my father's son in that regard. Thankfully."

"What will you do about this issue, Your Grace?"

Samuel smiled solemnly.

"I feel the need to unmask this anonymous writer."

"And how will you do that?"

A grin curled across Samuel's mouth, and his eyes sparkled in the sunlight that came from the large window that overlooked his country estate gardens. The late Duchess of Yarmouth had loved the gardens' lush greenery and immaculately kept flower beds. Although the gardener kept them still pristine, no one had set foot in those gardens since the Duchess' passing. They were not truly appreciated by the eyes and hands of those who maintained them. Samuel dared not enter the gardens, for there, the memories of his mother which still lingered in his heart would overwhelm him. He recalled sunny days when he and his mother would enjoy delightful picnics together, laughing and being happy. Those memories would remain forever with him, although he supposed that, with time, their intensity would fade, and the reminder of her passing would not be so painful.

A portrait of one of those many picnics hung in the gallery. His mother was depicted sitting on their most favored cotton blanket, with him sitting on her lap in the shadow of the large tree. It was a remarkable piece of art that he would never get rid of. Getting rid of it would be getting rid of a piece of his heart and soul - his very existence would be empty without it.

Samuel often sat in the gallery for hours, staring at the painting, recalling the smell of the flowers, the softness of the blanket, and the sound of his mother's voice, her laughter. Despite the painful memories of her passing, he did not wish to lose the joyous time they had spent together. Sunny days had a special place in his heart, as they reminded him of his late mother. But the winter months in the country made him miserable, and he needed distraction. Too many memories dwelled within the walls of Fletcher Hall, and those memories suffocated him. Fletcher Hall was his home and had been so for his entire life, but it had not been the same after his mother's passing, and even less so after his father's tragic end. He welcomed any form of distraction.

Searching for this man, who seemed to know more of him than he knew of himself, was the perfect excuse to leave Cornwall and its morose atmosphere. He no longer had the requirements of mourning to hold him here, and the sights of London might be precisely what he needed to lift his spirits, as well as to allow him to restore his reputation. But he would need to be careful, as he did not wish to ruin it more than it already had been tarnished by these scurrilous writings, and a single misstep might do that.

Samuel turned his gaze to Lord Felmar, who patiently awaited the Duke's response.

"I will return to London and find the true identity of this feebleminded gabster who cannot distinguish fact from fiction." Samuel stared at the letter resting on his desk, and his jaw clenched. "It was very courteous of Lord Timothy to bring this to my attention. He has always been a very close friend to me. If I inform him of my plan, I am confident that he will wish to join me on my quest to uncover the identity of the person who has so maligned me. After all, his constant presence in London will be of great advantage to me. He knows his way around the *ton* as well, far better than I do of late."

"Your Grace thinks that it is a member of the *ton* who has written this?" Lord Felmar asked.

"It must be. The writing gives the impression of an educated man. Although his foolish ways might count against him."

"And what will Your Grace do with the author of this article, supposing that you find them?"

"I have not quite decided yet, but this person, whomever it may be, has managed to have the whole *ton* question my reputation, and has brought shame to the good name of my family. That is something I will not stand for it. I will hunt him down."

"You think it wise to do so? It could be dangerous."

"Indeed. But I will not allow anyone to ruin my reputation in such a dishonorable manner. To publish such a thing anonymously is scurrilous!"

Samuel reached for the silver bell on his desk, irritated by the tension that had settled between his shoulders, and rang it vigorously. The door to the study opened slowly, and his butler appeared in the doorway.

"Your Grace."

He quietly awaited Samuel's response.

"Donnelly, I will be visiting London."

"When would Your Grace wish to depart?"

"As soon as possible."

"There is a storm coming. Must Your Grace travel in this abominable weather?"

The Duke narrowed his eyes at Donnelly and nodded.

"Yes, I must."

"Your Grace, I implore you-"

"Silence, Donnelly. I have decided, and my mind cannot be changed. Please inform all of the staff of my plans to depart for London. I wish to leave as soon as possible."

"Very well, Your Grace."

Donnelly left the study and closed the door behind him. Samuel drew in a deep breath and stared at the newspaper article that his good friend, Lord Timothy, had sent him, with a letter that explained what had been happening in his absence. Although Samuel still found it amusing that someone would dare attempt to sully the Fletcher name, he grew angry at the audacity of this man.

Or perhaps it was a woman?

But how on earth would a woman pen such things of him? Unless it was someone who knew him well. After all, one's enemies are frequently the ones who act as friends.

"I will unmask this man."

"First Your Grace must safely arrive in London."

"I am not afraid. Would you not do the same if you were in my position?"

Lord Felmar nodded, and Samuel felt confident that his actions were justified and not excessive.

CHAPTER TWO

"Oh, do stand up straight, Lillian."
Lady Lillian Colborne pursed her lips as her mother reminded her of her posture, despite her back being as straight as a fencing sword. Her posture was not the problem her mother had with Lillian. It was her second year in the marriage mart, and she had still not secured a match. It was utterly unacceptable to her mother that she was still unmarried. Every chance she had, she put pressure on Lillian, demanding that, somehow, she find a man to marry.

Arabella Colborne, Countess of Welsford, had ensured that her only daughter was raised to be a proper young lady who would easily find a husband, but the pickings were slim of late. During the past Season, however, several suitors had expressed interest in Lillian. Unfortunately, Lillian did not reciprocate their interest, much to her mother's dismay.

"I am, Mother. It is quite impossible to slouch in these stays that I parade in."

"I prefer to call it promenading, my dearest. In the public eye, we must always look our best, especially you."

"But the Season is over, Mother. I hardly think that any gentleman would be looking for a wife during these dreadful months."

"Need I remind you of the day that I met your father? Gallant and handsome, I caught his eye by being the most perfect young lady I could be, despite it being a miserable day."

Lillian pursed her lips, clasping her hands together inside the fur muff to hide her annoyance. She did not need to be reminded, as her mother constantly reminded her, of how perfect her parents' meeting was. Lillian was somewhat envious of it, as it was not a forced meeting where they both felt awkward and out of place, such as the many times her mother had introduced her to a possible suitor. Certainly, some of the gentlemen were handsome and well-mannered, but she did not feel a connection with any of them.

Lillian stared at the sky, and a solemn sigh escaped her throat. It was a cool and overcast winter afternoon, and it was certainly not helping with her complexion. The crisp air flushed the apples of her cheeks, giving her a childish appearance. That was certainly not what she needed.

"But why does it matter if I stand up straight? No one is looking. No one is even here at the park."

"You ought to be well aware that men adore women who stand up straight. It creates an air of sophistication and poise."

Where on earth had her mother heard such a preposterous thing? Men were not in the least bit interested in posture. They only wished to marry a young woman who came from a wealthy and reputable family, would adorn their arms at social events, and, of course, bear their children.

Lillian rolled her eyes subtly, turning her face away from her mother to prevent her from noticing Lillian's defiance. It was not that Lillian did not wish to be married, but rather that she wanted to choose her future husband, herself. Of course, her mother would not allow her to do so. She was twenty years old this year, and it had been two years since her presentation to society, which frustrated her mother to no end.

Now, her mother was more determined than ever to secure a match for her only daughter.

Lillian was envious of her older brother, Timothy, who was not under nearly as much pressure to marry as she was. Plus, he was older as well. She found it unfair that Timothy was able to live his life as a bachelor, attending a gentlemen's club and frolicking around the country as it pleased him.

Why was she not extended the same courtesy? She knew the answer, of course – it was because she was a woman.

A lady.

"What of Lord Bertram?" Lady Welsford asked suddenly.

Lillian's brow furrowed as she recalled Lord Bertram.

"Lord Bertram was ordinary. He had no knowledge of any of the books I have read."

Lady Welsford chuckled and shook her head.

"Oh, my dear. Men do not read the same things as we do. And you ought not to bore him with those novels you read."

"But I love them."

"Understandable, but you are not seeking the company of spinsters. You wish to attract a husband. Perhaps I should arrange for Lord Bertram to call."

Lillian forced a smile and knew that it was futile to argue with her mother.

"That sounds lovely, Mother." A chill ran up Lillian's spine as a gust of wind suddenly blew around her and Lady Welsford. "The wind is starting to pick up. Shall we head back to the carriage?"

"Before we do that, may I say something?"

Lillian glanced at her mother, and her brow furrowed in both intrigue and confusion. It was not like her mother to withhold things from her, but the expression on her mother's face suggested otherwise.

"Of course. Is something the matter, Mother?"

"Not at all. I am merely trying to do my best for you, Lillian. I want you to have the best life possible. And I am more than aware that finding a husband is the last thing on your own list of priorities, but it is important to me, and your father."

"And our family as well."

"Precisely, my dear," Lady Welsford murmured as she gently touched Lillian's cheek. "For generations, the Colborne family has prided itself on its impeccable reputation. Our marriages have lasted lifetimes, with no unpleasantness, and we have produced heirs to keep the family going, or the families we marry into, for the daughters."

"And I am failing to fulfill that by not being married yet."

Lillian lowered her gaze with regret. She knew of her family and its history, but she had not realized how important it was to her mother. Her father never badgered her with these things, as he was a man of few words. As many people described him, he was the strong, silent type, and it was the truth. But when he spoke, people paid attention, as it would be something important.

And while Lord Welsford commanded authority, he was kind and gentle in Lillian's company. Perhaps it was because Lillian was his only daughter, and he had a very special place in his heart for her.

"It is not that, but finding a husband is good. Finding the *right* husband is better."

"And how do I know who is the right one?"

"We don't unless it is a love match, and those are rather rare. But Lord Bertram is a good man. He comes from a family which has both wealth and influence. I believe he also attended Oxford."

Lillian's eyes sparkled with interest, and she pointed out, "Perhaps Timothy might know him."

"I already asked, but your brother was vague with his answer."

"Perhaps he is aware of something you are not, Mother."

"Do not say such things, Lillian."

Lady Welsford stared sternly at Lillian, working her

lower lip anxiously. She did not intend to upset her mother, especially not when it came to suitors. Or her brother, for that matter. He was the apple of her eye.

"Where *is* Timothy? Was he not supposed to join us this afternoon?"

Lady Welsford fobbed Lillian off and shook her head.

"Your brother would rather be anywhere else than keep his mother and sister company, it seems."

"It must be nice to do whatever one pleases," Lillian muttered.

"Do not mumble, dear."

"Oh, it was nothing important, Mother."

As she looked into the distance, across the park, which was now covered by a light whisper of snow, Lillian's eye followed the stone pathway and she noticed her older brother, Timothy, strolling towards them. Timothy exuded confidence and charm when wearing his usual attire of dark breeches, black boots, a dark jacket with an emerald-green cravat, and a bright smile.

The young ladies of the *ton*, as well as their mamas, adored Timothy, but he had not shown significant interest in any of them, and of course, courting was out of the question. Despite his age of six and twenty, he had no thought of marriage, and Lillian's mother uttered not a single word about it. It was infuriating to Lillian, as she had been pestered nonstop since her Come Out. Perhaps, like her brother, she also did not wish to be married. But of course, no one listened to her.

"Timothy, my darling."

Lillian watched as Lady Welsford beamed at Timothy, embracing him lovingly. Timothy winked at Lillian and eventually pulled away from his mother.

"Mother. My dear sister. Are you enjoying your stroll?" he asked, his eyes sparkling with amusement.

He was well aware of how much Lillian despised these strolls with their mother. It was as though she was put on show like a prize calf, ready for the slaughter.

"It is lovely. In fact, we were speaking of you a few moments ago."

"You were?" Timothy asked and cocked his head at Lillian.

"Indeed. Mother wishes to arrange for Lord Bertram to call, and I want to know if he is a good suitor."

Timothy shifted his weight rather uncomfortably and his jaw clenched. He appeared nervous and swallowed hard.

"Perhaps Lillian should refrain from seeking a husband in such dreary conditions. It does nothing for her complexion. Wait until Spring, rather, for the sunbeams to add some color to her porcelain skin."

Lillian's jaw dropped, and she stared at Timothy. She was not certain whether to be shocked by his words or welcome them with open arms. She would be forever grateful to him if he could convince their mother to postpone her matchmaking for Lillian until the Spring - if anyone had that power and influence, it would be Timothy.

"Never in my life have I heard such fustian nonsense. Wherever did that come from, Timothy?"

Timothy shrugged his shoulders and glanced around.

"It does seem rather pointless. It is winter and so close to Christmas. And speaking of Christmas-"

"Timothy, apologies for interrupting, but what of Lord Bertram?"

Lady Welsford sounded, most unusually, actually a little annoyed with Timothy.

"Is he not too old for Lillian?"

"He is the same age as you are."

"That is precisely my point. Would she not fare better with a gentleman her own age?"

"That is not how this works, Timothy. You ought to know this."

Lillian's gaze moved back and forth between her mother and her brother. They spoke of her as though she was not standing beside them, and it was infuriating.

"Do I not get a say in this?" Lillian interjected.

Both her mother and brother paused for a moment and turned to her.

"*Do* you want a say in this, sister?"

"At least a little," she answered, wringing her hands together inside her muff.

"Perhaps Timothy is right," Lady Welsford sighed theatrically. "Perhaps we ought to hold off for a while, until the new year, at least. I will consider it."

Lillian gazed at Timothy gratefully but lowered her gaze before her mother could notice.

"What were you going to say about Christmas, my darling?" Lady Welsford asked Timothy.

"Oh, yes. A very good friend of mine, whom I met while at Oxford, is returning to London soon. Would it be alright if he joined us for Christmas? He has no other family, and I do not wish him to spend Christmastide alone."

Lady Welsford and Lillian exchanged puzzled and intrigued glances, and Lady Welsford asked, "Who is this friend?"

"We attended university together in Oxford, as I mentioned."

Timothy grinned, his shoulders straight, his hands behind his back.

Lady Welsford's eyes narrowed curiously.

"You have never introduced us to this friend, have you?"

"I have not. But he and I have exchanged letters for a while. He is managing his estate in Cornwall but is traveling to London to visit me. Please, Mother. I consider him family, and to him, I am the only family he has," Timothy uttered.

"Very well, but I will consult with your father when we arrive home."

"Wonderful."

As Lillian watched her brother, she noticed something strange in his behavior. He had been very vague when he spoke of his friend and had not even given his friend's name. Who was this friend of Timothy's, and why was he doing his best to keep his name a secret?

Lillian bit her lower lip as she wondered what her brother was hiding since she had never truly seen him act this way before.

But, in her experience, the festive cheer of Christmas did rather strange things to even the most normal of people, Timothy included. Perhaps it was just that.

CHAPTER THREE

"I have missed these streets," Samuel softly pondered as his carriage drove through the streets of London.

Traveling from Cornwall had been grueling for him, as the snow and cold weather had made the journey difficult and longer than expected. Traveling such long distances in the winter was not ideal, but there was no other option, except to travel by sea, which could be just as uncomfortable. But he endured it, for he wished to unmask the man who had written such terrible things about him, spreading untruths and tainting his reputation.

That person was going to pay dearly.

The journey to London had taken six days, and Samuel was more than ready to leave the confines of his coach and step onto the cobblestones in front of his townhouse in Mayfair. He had not set foot in his London home in a long while, and it would be lovely to settle in, even if it was only temporary. He was not certain how long he would stay in London, but luckily his good friend, Lord Timothy, would be there to keep him company.

As the familiar sights of Mayfair came into view through the windows of the coach, Samuel smiled slightly, already feeling more at home. His absence from London had been too long, but he still felt as though he belonged in the city, surrounded by its wealth and people.

The coach came to a stop, and his footman's voice could be heard from outside.

"We have arrived, Your Grace."

"Very good," Samuel replied.

Within a few moments, the footman opened the coach door, and let down the steps, allowing Samuel to step outside. The air was brisk, and colder than he remembered London being, but luckily, he wore his winter coat, as the countryside was even colder than the city.

He nodded at the footman with gratitude and gazed up at his townhouse. Everything still appeared as it had the last time he was there, and he was unexpectedly filled with nostalgia. The remnants of snow crunched under his boots as he walked up the steps.

The front door opened, and he saw Billings, the butler, and not far behind him, Mrs. Hall, the Housekeeper, standing in the foyer.

Billings bowed, and Mrs Hall curtsied. Billings had been with the family since Samuel was a young boy, and, while Mrs. Hall had not been with them that long, she had been the housekeeper from before Samuel had inherited his title, and was well-known in the family for her diligence, hard work, and discretion. She had certainly encountered many things requiring discretion in her lifetime and had managed to keep them within the walls of the townhouse. She was a stout woman of middle-age, but highly dependable, and had given Samuel a wealth of advice during his life.

"Welcome home, Your Grace," she greeted him with a polite smile.

"You will find all in readiness, Your Grace."

Billings smiled as the Duke stepped further into the house, and footmen scurried to go out and remove his luggage from the coach.

"Thank you, Billings, Mrs. Hall."

"It is wonderful to have you back, Your Grace. We prepared for your arrival over the last week, and have readied a lovely dinner for you."

Samuel nodded.

"I do not have much of an appetite, Mrs. Hall. It must be due to the long journey. Perhaps later."

"Very well, Your Grace. I will have your luggage sent up to your rooms immediately. Is your valet with you?"

"Helms will be here shortly – he is following in the second coach, with the rest of my luggage."

With that, Samuel turned and retreated to the drawing room for some privacy, having no wish to be in his rooms while all of his luggage was being unpacked. The drawing room was still as light and welcoming as he remembered. There were elegant soft furnishings, exquisitely carved items of furniture, and a beautiful harp that stood in the corner. His mother had loved to play the instrument and after her death, Samuel had not had the heart to get rid of it, so it stood now in the drawing room, upon a Brussels weave carpet with a backdrop of mauve and gold-adorned wallpaper. The rich colors gave a feeling of great luxury, as the late Duchess had adored all things exquisite. Samuel could practically see her seated at the harp, her delicate fingers gently tugging at the strings. Angelic music would fill the air, and the room would be even more enchanting when lit, at night, by the glittering light cast from the ornate chandeliers.

A smile crossed his lips, but only briefly, as sadness filled his heart. It was at times such as these that Samuel wished for her guidance. She had been wise and beautiful, and it pained him very much that he did not have her in his world any longer. He approached the harp, wishing that he had the skill to play his mother's favorite melody, but he knew that he did not. His silence was interrupted by footsteps echoing through the hallway, and a light knock on the drawing room door.

"Your Grace?"

Samuel whirled around and stared at the footman.

"Yes?"

"Pardon the interruption, Your Grace. This letter was delivered for you," he announced. Samuel noticed the letter in his hand.

Samuel's brow furrowed, and he approached the footman.

"When was this delivered?"

"Mere moments ago, Your Grace. It was delivered by an errand boy, who simply said that the sender was a gentleman."

"Thank you."

Samuel took the letter from the footman, who bowed and left the room, then opened the letter.

From the very first line, Samuel's jaw clenched at the words. It was from the person who had fabricated those lies about him and spoke of his handiwork so far, and his mission to ruin Samuel and his perfect reputation. With every word he read, Samuel became angrier and could not believe the audacity of this person.

Who did they think they were?

No one was allowed to speak to a Duke in such a manner, much less taunt him the way that the author of this letter had done. It was unacceptable and, in his anger, he balled up the letter in his hands and threw it onto the floor. Stepping away, his heart pounding fiercely in his chest, Samuel knew that he had to find the person responsible, and fast.

After a moment, he retrieved the crumpled letter, smoothed it out, and examined it closely.

Unfortunately, and as expected, the letter did not contain a name or any indication of who was behind this. This did not deter Samuel in any way, but it did make it harder to discover who was behind it – for a moment there, he had held out a slight hope that the letter might provide a clue. Still, he was determined to find the culprit.

Drawing in a few strained breaths, Samuel rushed out of the drawing room, calling for Billings. Once the butler appeared, he asked that the town carriage be brought around.

"I must go to Brooks' immediately."

"Very well, Your Grace."

He went back to the drawing room and retrieved the crumpled letter. He would need evidence to track down this gossip.

A short while later, Samuel's jaw clenched as he stepped up into his smaller carriage, which did not carry the ducal escutcheon, for he generally preferred to remain inconspicuous. He did not wish to make a fuss over his return or suggest that he was on his way to Brooks' to gamble, as the letter made clear that the sender suggested he did. Gambling had never been one of Samuel's vices, as he was impatient and did not possess the skill to win any card games. Yet, according to the slandering writer, he had frequented gentlemen's clubs and was in financial ruin due to his gambling.

The truth was far from it.

Once the carriage stopped in front of Brooks', Samuel climbed out and entered the Palladian style yellow brick and Portland stone building. He was welcomed by the establishment's staff and received numerous nods of acknowledgment. He was rather surprised at this since the tales of his supposed gambling had been made public. He reciprocated the gestures and waved over a footman, ordering his usual drink of choice, malt whisky.

"Yarmouth, is that you?"

A familiar voice spun him from his angered mood, and he glanced over his shoulder, to see the approach of his very good friend, Lord Timothy Colborne. It had been Lord Timothy who had informed him of this whole mess of apparent scandals occurring in London in his absence, and Samuel considered Lord Timothy a true friend for keeping him apprised of what was happening.

The two men had met when they attended Oxford University, and their friendship had stood the test of time and distance since. Each time that they met again, it did not feel as though they had spent any time apart. Their association was filled with ease and comfort, which Samuel greatly appreciated. Any moment where he was able to be himself without any pretense, was a fine moment indeed.

Samuel greeted Lord Timothy with a solid handshake and smiled.

"It is very good to see you, my friend."

"Likewise. I was not expecting you to arrive for another few days."

The gentlemen took their seats in the leather chairs at a nearby table and Lord Timothy grinned at him.

"You made the trip from Cornwall in remarkable time."

"It was not without its challenges, I assure you."

"I presume the content of my recent letter is what has brought you to London so hastily?"

"Indeed. I require your assistance."

"What kind of assistance?"

Samuel leaned forward and hushed his voice.

"You have always been keen on mysteries, have you not?"

"Yes, indeed."

Lord Timothy narrowed his eyes at Samuel, not quite certain what he would say next.

"I require your help to unmask this crazed gossiper who insists on mocking me and threatening to ruin my reputation."

"I do not understand – have they done something more than just publish that article?"

The Duke took a large swallow of his drink and placed the empty glass on the table. He retrieved the letter from his coat and passed it to Lord Timothy.

"I received this letter from this person at my townhouse in Mayfair shortly after my arrival today."

Lord Timothy's brow furrowed as he examined the letter

"How on earth did they know that you were to arrive today? Not even I knew."

"That is the question, my friend. Perhaps he gave someone a coin to wait and watch until I arrived at the townhouse."

Lord Timothy cocked his head but did not appear convinced.

"Perhaps."

"Please, help me in my pursuit of this gossip, Colborne."

Samuel despised begging since he would never force anyone into helping him if they did not wish to, but he had no other option.

"Of course I will help you. You are my friend, Yarmouth. And speaking of being my friend, do you have plans for Christmas?"

"Christmas in London was not in my plans at all, but here I am," Samuel stated and ran his finger along the rim of the empty glass. "Why do you ask?"

Lord Timothy's face lit up, and he grinned widely.

"Then you must join my family and me for the holiday, starting with dinner the day after tomorrow. Our chef prepares the best goose, which I am certain you will love."

Samuel pondered only for a moment.

"I do enjoy a well-prepared goose. Would I not be imposing on your family's celebration?"

Lord Timothy waved a hand, dismissing his objection.

"Of course not. They are looking forward to meeting you."

Samuel shifted in his chair and rested his hand against his cheek.

"You have not consulted them, have you?"

"I have, but I may have been vague when they inquired of your identity."

"Would the rumors of my supposed indiscretions and antics have anything to do with your vagueness?"

"My apologies, Yarmouth. It is not that I am ashamed of you, nor do I believe those rumors for a moment, but you must understand something. My mother's adamance on the matter of keeping our family reputation as stainless as possible is very strong. My father, on the other hand, will welcome you with open arms since I have spoken of you to him many times, and although he has not met you, he already thinks highly of you."

Samuel sighed.

"That is certainly a relief. I would not wish to upset your mother or any member of your family. And I do not wish them to be upset with you either."

"Do not fret, old friend. I will explain the situation to my parents first thing on the morrow. My father is very understanding, and I will make it clear that the rumors of you are not true."

"You are a good friend, Colborne."

Lord Timothy smiled brightly and rose to his feet.

"Another drink?"

"That would be lovely."

Samuel and Lord Timothy spent the rest of the night conversing and sharing stories of all that had occurred whilst they had been away from one another. Despite being apart for so long, it felt, as it usually did between them, as though no time had passed since they had last been together. Between the walls of Brooks', the two friends became reacquainted as their friendship strengthened, and Samuel felt more at home than ever in London.

CHAPTER FOUR

"I do love this color on her."

Lillian stared at her reflection in the mirror - she was wearing an unfinished dress in a lovely shade of pale blue. The modiste pinned the dress to fit the silhouette of her bust perfectly, allowing the skirt to hang freely around her. The soft material swished as it moved and gently caressed her arms which were hanging at her sides.

"It suits her very well, my Lady."

The modiste smiled at Lady Welsford and winked at Lillian in the mirror's reflection.

The modiste, Madame Periaux, had a talent for transforming rolls of silks, cotton, and lace into the most exquisite gowns, and has even created the occasional pair of shoes as well. She had told Lillian and Lady Welsford that her father was a cobbler, and he had taught her how to fashion shoes and boots. She did make elegant evening slippers upon request, but her forte was stylish gowns and day dresses for her clientele, who were solely members of the *ton*. Her prices were high, but with it came social status, and being seen in a creation that came from her shop held a certain prestige.

Ever since Lillian was a young girl, she and her mother had visited Madame Periaux's, and the modiste had never disappointed. Her dresses were of high quality, and she took pride in her creations, as she knew the *ton* were difficult to please. She always delivered the perfect gown.

"I do love it as well. It will suit me even better as soon as this dreary winter ends. I cannot wait for the Spring to arrive," Lillian uttered, eyeing herself in the mirror.

Her golden hair was pinned up and to the side, and then tumbled down past her shoulder in one thick curl, with wisps of golden locks framing her face.

"Are you hoping to catch the eye of a certain gentleman next Season, Lady Lillian?" Madame Periaux inquired with a broad smile.

Lillian was on the verge of answering the question when her mother interjected.

"Perhaps sooner. It will be Lillian's third Season, and prospects will start to thin as new ladies make their Come Outs in society."

"I cannot believe it has already been three Seasons since your Come Out, Lady Lillian."

"Indeed it has. I do feel the need to double my efforts to secure Lillian a match, possibly before the Season opens."

"If it is anyone who has the tenacity to succeed, it is most certainly you, my Lady."

Lillian wrinkled her nose, as her mother's words left a

bitter taste in her mouth. She had hoped that she would have met someone who she found interesting, and who made her feel seen in an ocean of young women, but the ballrooms were crowded, and the mamas were relentless in their pursuit of finding their daughters a match.

It was a great fear of Lillian's that she might have somehow missed her love match, that she had not noticed him hiding in the corner of a ballroom, or perhaps concealed in an alcove, not wishing to be spotted by the scouting mamas. Perhaps he had been on the verge of approaching her, only to be intimidated by the gentlemen who attempted to impress her with their boasting.

Lillian bit her lower lip, hoping that this was not true and that her love match was still roaming the streets, determined to find her. But she was constantly reminded by her mother that love matches were rare and that she should not depend on that possibility. Many fine gentlemen in London were seeking wives, and she should not hold out for a love match.

But how could she not hope for love? How could she agree to marry a man she did not love? Was that not the ultimate injustice? Or rather the ultimate punishment? How could she learn to love a man who she did not feel any attraction towards? She had certainly found many of the gentlemen whom she had been introduced to to be handsome and charming, but none of them felt right. Of course, her mother thought that she was being preposterous in saying such things.

This was why her mother was set on arranging a call from Lord Bertram. He was certainly handsome, and slightly older than Lillian, but he came from a wealthy and influential family. Although Lillian had not spent much time in his company, he was a delightful dancer, and he was well-spoken. And of course, he had attended Oxford University, which made him not only well-schooled but also intelligent. Perhaps she ought to give Lord Bertram a chance to prove himself. After all, being the wife of a Marquess was better than being a spinster.

"I wonder what color Lord Bertram prefers," Lillian blurted out.

Lady Welsford stared at her for a moment, rendered speechless, but a satisfied smile appeared on her lips shortly after the shock had settled.

"Perhaps we ought to ask him."

Lillian nodded quietly. She did not wish to fight with her mother, especially not when it was about suitors. She did not stand a chance, as her mother ruled Welsford-House and all those who lived under its roof, with an iron fist

"Lord Bertram, the Marquess?" Madame Periaux inquired.

"Indeed."

"I have heard that he is quite handsome, and he attended Oxford. He sounds like a very fine match, Miss Colborne."

"We shall see," Lillian smiled slightly.

From the far corner of the store, two young women were heard, despite their attempts to keep their voices hushed.

"Did you hear that he has returned to London?"

"I am quite surprised that he dared to show his face here, after all the rumors about his antics."

"Are you certain that those are true?"

"Why would they not be true? His Grace does frequent Brooks'. He was seen there again last night with a friend of his."

"Why would he frequent such places if he is financially ruined? And for that matter, where would he get the resources to travel to London from his estate in the countryside?"

Lillian's brow furrowed and she turned to her mother.

"Who are they speaking of?"

"Does it matter?"

"Of course it does."

Lillian stepped down from the pedestal before Madame Periaux and Lady Welsford were able to stop her.

"Lillian..." Lady Welsford hissed, but she ignored her mother.

Lillian approached the two young women, who were approximately her age, and cleared her throat.

"Pardon me for the very abrupt intrusion, ladies, but who do you speak of?"

The two young ladies were stunned momentarily and stared at Lillian. After they regained their composure, one motioned to Lillian's half-finished dress.

"That certainly is a lovely color on you."

"Thank you," Lillian nodded. "I do apologize for asking, but I could not help but overhear part of your conversation. Who were you two speaking of a moment ago?"

"The Duke of Yarmouth."

"He has been frequenting Brooks' gentlemen's club and has gambled away his fortune, so it is said."

"It is also said that he was spotted in various *undesirable* haunts here in London, with Haymarket ware."

"What does that mean?" Lillian asked.

"He was seen in the company of Birds of Paradise."

Lillian's brow furrowed and she shook her head. Still not understanding.

"Brothels, of course."

Lillian cringed and was taken aback by the harsh word that the young woman had used, but she now understood what she spoke of. Lillian was not allowed to bring up such improper topics, despite her knowing that Timothy frequented Brooks' as well. He would often parade into Welsford House, more than a little half-sprung, at ghastly times of the evening, or rather the morning. She could only imagine what her mother would say if she was aware of what he did. But then again, she would do nothing, or Timothy would get off very lightly. He always did.

"Where did you hear all of this?" Lillian inquired with a frown.

"Do you not read the newspaper?"

"A whole article was written about the Duke."

"That's probably why he is visiting London."

"Was he not residing in London before the article?"

Lillian cocked her head to the side.

The two young ladies exchanged puzzled glances and shook their heads.

"He resides in the countryside most of the time, apparently."

"Hiding away from the *ton* because of his shameful actions."

Lillian was still puzzled.

"But why would he return to London?"

"You ask many questions."

Lillian shrugged.

"My mother tells me that on numerous occasions."

"Lillian, come here at once."

Lillian cringed as her mother suddenly appeared beside her.

"Mother, I was merely inquiring-"

"That is quite enough. Proper young ladies such as yourselves should not be concerned with such gossip, especially not about disgraceful men."

"Do you know the Duke of Yarmouth, my Lady?"

Lady Welsford's eyes widened, and a vein began throbbing in her temple, which Lillian found rather odd. Did her mother know the Duke of Yarmouth? If she did, how did she know him?

"Men such as the Duke of Yarmouth give a bad name to their families and all people associated with them. Merely speaking his name taints your reputations, which is not what young ladies such as yourself need."

Lady Welsford wrapped her hand around Lillian's wrist and practically dragged her back to where Madame Periaux waited for them.

"Mother, you did not need to manhandle me so roughly," Lillian complained as she rubbed her bruised arm.

"I will do whatever is required to keep your reputation as flawless as it needs to be, Lillian."

The air was filled with tension inside the dress shop, and even the two young women Lillian had approached were silent.

"Mother, I was merely asking who they spoke of. You have never stopped me from listening to gossip before. Why are you so affected by the antics of the Duke of Yarmouth?"

Lady Welsford appeared even more angered by Lillian's question, much to Lilian's confusion. Her mother's actions and overreaction seemed unnecessary and suspicious.

"Do not waste your breath on men of that kind. Your attention should be focused on finding a husband, or I shall do it for you. Now, allow Madame Periaux to continue adjusting your gown, Lillian."

Lillian narrowed her eyes, staring at her mother, but did as she was told before her mother rang a fine peal over her. She felt embarrassed enough and did not need to feel any more humiliated. With colored cheeks, Lillian nodded and turned back to Madame Periaux, who appeared as uncomfortable as she was.

The seamstress smiled and turned to Lady Welsford.

"Perhaps some tea, my Lady?" she offered.

Lady Welsford sighed theatrically and pressed her hand to her forehead.

"That would be lovely. Thank you."

Madame Periaux ordered her assistant to bring tea, and within a few moments, the young woman brought out a tea tray and offered tea to Lady Welsford. When she lifted it from the tray, the porcelain cup clattered against the saucer, clearly indicating the extent of Lady Welsford's distress.

Lillian stepped onto the small stand again, and Madame Periaux continued adjusting the fabric of her bodice. She stared into the mirror at her mother's reflection, watching her nervously sip the cup of tea, and her brow furrowed.

Why was her mother so shaken by the gossip of the Duke of Yarmouth? And why did she not wish Lillian to engage in that gossip? She had never pulled Lillian away so harshly before, and gossiping was something that Lady Welsford did not mind at all, usually, as it brought information, and she knew that Lillian did not enjoy sharing gossip, so would not spread it further.

As Lillian continued to watch her mother in the mirror subtly, she realized that this could only mean one thing; that her mother personally knew of the Duke of Yarmouth, and was greatly affected by these rumors.

But how?

Lillian was fully aware that her mother would not be the one to reveal that to her, which made her even more adamant about finding out for herself. Perhaps Timothy would be able to assist. After all, he knew how to wrap their mother around his finger.

CHAPTER FIVE

"*G*ood afternoon, ladies."

Samuel tipped his top hat at the small group of young women who strolled past him, and their cheeks immediately colored.

"Good afternoon, Your Grace."

The young women reciprocated his greeting, but before they could utter another word, their concerned mamas immediately rushed towards them. Judging by the expressions on their faces, it was clear that they were well aware of the rumors floating around Town about him.

"I never thought I would see the day when you would be considered undesirable, Yarmouth," Lord Perkins pointed out.

As well as Lord Timothy, Lord Perkins was a close friend of Samuel's. Their parents were old friends, and they had grown up together. It had been a long while since Samuel and Lord Perkins had seen one another, and it was enjoyable to spend time together again, even it if were only on an afternoon stroll through Mayfair. On this day, Lord Timothy was otherwise engaged with his family, which was why he had not joined the two gentlemen in their stroll.

Out of the corner of Samuel's eye, he noticed people staring at him. Some more subtly than others, some shamelessly staring with angry and disgusted scowls, while others made no attempt to speak in hushed tones as they passed.

Of course, the mamas rushed to their daughters to keep them as far away from Samuel as possible. The mere thought of having them within speaking distance of the Duke might taint their reputations and render them ruined.

"Only undesirable to those who know of the rumors," Samuel pointed out.

Unaffected by the mamas' scowls, Samuel tipped his hat at them as they scurried away. He found it quite amusing that a rumor had the power to change people's behavior to such a degree. Never in his life had he experienced something like this before, and it amused him to no end. Of course, it angered him as well, as the person responsible was still at large, and Samuel had yet to speak with Lord Timothy about their strategy to catch the author of that damaging article.

But for now, Samuel relished the attention, regardless of if it was good or bad.

"That may be all the people in London at this point in time, Your Grace," Lord Perkins chuckled.

"Yet you still remain by my side."

"That is entirely different. You are my friend, and it

is not as though *I* wish to marry you," Lord Perkins stated.

"That is true. How is the lovely Lady Perkins?"

"She is well. She apologized for not joining us on our stroll. She had to accompany her mother to visit an elderly friend who had taken ill."

"I see."

"It has nothing to do with you and your supposed antics, Yarmouth."

"Are you certain?"

Lord Perkins nodded.

"Indeed I am. It strikes me as odd that it affects you the way it does. Was it not you who said that you did not care what others thought of you."

"That was before my name was slandered by an anonymous writer who attempted to pass off fiction as facts."

"He certainly succeeded."

"I wish to unmask him," Samuel said, smiling politely at passersby.

"And then what?" Lord Perkins inquired.

"Then my reputation can be restored. I do not appreciate the scowls and stares I am receiving, although the mamas' reactions do amuse me."

"And it will ensure that you can secure a match without being rejected," Lord Perkins uttered, but there was a questioning tone in his voice.

Samuel's brow furrowed, and he was silent for a moment.

"That is not why I came to London. Finding a wife is not a priority to me, at least not now."

"If you wish, I could introduce you to a few of my wife's friends."

Samuel scoffed.

"You will do no such thing."

Lord Perkins chuckled.

"Or perhaps I should wait for your reputation to be restored."

"Perhaps that is a wise choice."

Samuel's jaw tightened, as his mind became cloudy with thoughts. He had not considered finding a wife or entertained the idea of marrying. Although, it would not be as lonely at his estate in Cornwall if he were to take a wife. The longer the rumors were being spread by the *ton* and taken as the truth, the smaller the chances of him finding a young woman whose mama would allow her daughter to marry him.

He was not even certain what type of young lady he would be interested in.

"It is not something I have thought of, Perkins," Samuel uttered as he stared at the path in front of him. "I am aware that I am six-and-twenty, but surely that does not mean that I must marry as soon as possible."

"With all due respect, Your Grace, it is not as though you are being pressured to marry by your parents. You are a man who is allowed to decide your own fate."

"Indeed. I recall my mother telling me that I could search as hard as I wished for the right person, but I would not find her. Fate will bring her to me, and she will fall in my lap when the time is right."

"I do hope she did not mean that in a literal sense."

Samuel and Lord Perkins chuckled at his comment and Samuel cleared his throat.

"Until that happens, I will focus my attention on finding the gabster who insists on ruining my reputation."

"You are a resourceful man, after all. It will be easy for you."

"Thank you, my friend."

The two men found their way to Mayfair's busiest street, filled with young women and their mothers, young couples who lovingly batted their lashes at each other, and carriages that awaited their passengers returning from the tearooms, the modistes, and the bakery. Footmen loaded trunks of new gowns onto the carriages, and maids followed young ladies as they made their way about.

The street was lively, but attention shifted towards Samuel as he and Lord Perkins crossed the street. People stepped back, as though he carried a disease which they were afraid he would pass on to them. Luckily, Samuel was not affected by that and politely nodded at them. He and Lord Perkins came to a stop on the side of the street, and he turned to his friend.

"Since you are in Town, how are you spending Christmas? You are welcome to join Catherine and I but, be warned, her mother does tend to be a trifle disguised during this festive time of the year."

"As entertaining as that sounds, Perkins, I must decline. Lord Timothy invited me to spend Christmas with his family," Samuel explained with a cringing expression.

"And Lady Welsford agreed to this?"

Lord Perkins was obviously surprised at the news.

Samuel shrugged and shifted his weight from side to side.

"He assured me that there would not be any issues. He would simply explain that the tales of my antics were not true."

"And that would be enough to persuade his mother? You ought to know how Lady Welsford is."

"I also know that Lord Timothy is his mother's favorite, and he can practically get away with anything," Samuel answered.

"Let us hope that is true. The Colbornes are a lovely family, although Lady Welsford can be rather protective of her daughter."

"Yes, of course. Lord Timothy's younger sister. I have yet to meet her, even though Lord Timothy has already urged me to stay away from her."

"From what I have heard, she is a very intelligent and witty young lady, and she will see right through your charming facade," Lord Perkins grinned. "I am fairly certain that she will put you in your place before you have the chance to charm her."

Samuel pressed his hand against his chest and feigned anguish.

"Your words wound me, old friend."

Lord Perkins laughed heartily and slid his golden pocket watch out of his pocket.

"Good heavens. I must be going."

"Very well. It was delightful catching up with you. We must do so again. Perhaps you can join me and Lord Timothy at Brooks' one evening. If Catherine allows it, of course," Samuel suggested with a playful grin.

"Wait until you are married, Yarmouth. You will want to spend all of your time with your beloved."

"That remains to be seen. Good day, Perkins," Samuel nodded and tipped his hat at his friend.

"Good day, Yarmouth. Do not get into too much trouble."

"I cannot promise anything."

Samuel winked and watched as Lord Perkins turned on his heel and hastily strutted back the way they had come. He cocked his head and wondered whether he would truly marry one day, but he could not imagine it. It seemed rather out of reach for him at that moment, and not only because he was the most undesirable man in Town.

Samuel continued his stroll along the street, as the people around him either did not notice him anymore, or he was not considered important enough to avoid any longer. The door of a nearby modiste opened, and golden hair sparkling in the little bit of winter sun caught his attention immediately. It belonged to a beautiful young lady who he had never seen before, despite feeling a sense of familiarity when he gazed upon her. She wore a dark blue day dress with long sleeves, lace trim, and a fur muff around her hands. Her cheeks were flushed from the fresh cold air, but her beautiful smile was what caused him to abruptly stop in his tracks. He had never laid eyes upon such a radiant smile in his entire life. The fact that it belonged to such a beauty was a bonus.

He simply had to speak to her, but he was certain that

her mama would follow her shortly from the dress shop, as she looked too young to be married already.

Or at least, so Samuel hoped.

The young lady stepped onto the pavement, and their gazes met for a brief moment. Even though it was only for a moment, Samuel felt a stir from within him. The attraction he felt towards this unknown young lady was stronger than he had ever felt in his entire life to any woman, and he carefully approached her. He did not wish to move too quickly, as he did not wish to startle her. Young women of the *ton* were fragile little things who could shatter like glass, he was once told by a friend. It was not true in all cases but in most.

As he approached her, she seemed distracted and did not see the step in front of her. A sense of urgency filled Samuel, and he rushed towards her. He reached his arms out and caught her as she misjudged the step and lost her balance. Samuel's arms wrapped around her delicate frame, and he was afraid his grasp would be too tight, but he could not let go.

The young lady gasped as Samuel caught her, preventing her from falling to the ground, and her eyes widened from both shock and relief. An intoxicating scent of wildflowers and lavender filled the air around Samuel, and the sweet scent caused his nose to tingle. Or perhaps it was the warmth of the young woman in his arms. The young lady recovered her balance and pushed away from him until she stood upright. Her cheeks colored a deep red from embarrassment and she stared at Samuel.

"My sincerest apologies."

"There is no need for an apology, my Lady. Are you well?"

The young woman nodded tightly, smoothing the skirt of her dress. Her fur muff lay on the ground, and Samuel bent to retrieve it. Straightening up, he handed the muff back to the young woman, and her gaze lowered shyly.

"Thank you. You are very kind."

"Are you certain that you are well?"

"Indeed. It was merely an accident. I did not realize that step was so far from my reach. But I am well, despite a hint of humiliation."

"You have nothing to be humiliated about. Luckily, I was here to catch you."

"Indeed. My luck was not entirely terrible."

A smile formed upon Samuel's lips as he intently gazed at the young woman, her bright eyes sparkling in the sunlight, her golden hair framing her face like a halo.

Who was this beautiful young woman who had quite literally fallen at his feet?

CHAPTER SIX

Oh my.
Lillian's heart pounded in her chest as the handsome gentleman before her stared intently at her. His hazel eyes were mesmerizing and warm. The manly scent of him had created a whirlwind of fluttering inside her stomach. His mere presence brought forth many curious feelings, but a sense of overwhelming excitement as well. Her racing heart was evident enough to create curiosity inside her.

Who was this man?

Why was his gaze so alluring to Lillian?

And why could she not utter a single word without her cheeks coloring?

This gentleman had rescued her from humiliation, although she felt incredibly foolish. She was not a clumsy young lady under normal circumstances, but she had never been that close to a man before. They had not even been properly introduced, and already she had imagined their future together. It was rather presumptuous of her to imagine such things from only meeting someone so swiftly, but Lillian could not help herself. Those thoughts were overwhelming and quite remarkable.

Lillian's brow furrowed as she composed herself and straightened her shoulders.

"Thank you for your assistance. It would have been rather embarrassing if I had fallen."

"It was my absolute pleasure. Allow me to introduce myself. I am-"

"Perhaps you ought to keep your introductions to yourself," Lillian heard her mother utter rather rudely, and she looked at her over her shoulder to see that Lady Welsford's cheeks were colored, but it was not from embarrassment. Her eyes flashed angrily, and she wrapped her fingers around Lillian's arm. "We must go," she hissed at Lillian and pulled her in the opposite direction from the gentleman.

"Mother, wait. This kind gentleman saved me from a potentially humiliating fate. I missed the step and I-"

"Perhaps you should watch where you are walking, dear."

Lillian's brow furrowed at her mother's tone, and she turned to the gentleman.

"Pardon my mother."

Before she could apologize to the gentleman, Lady Welsford pulled Lillian's arm with more vigor and forced her in the opposite direction. The two ladies crossed the road and Lady Welsford almost shoved Lillian into their carriage. She watched as her mother settled opposite her, and felt almost smothered inside the confined space with her suddenly rather rude and unpleasant mother.

"What is wrong, Mother? Why were you rude to that gentleman?"

"That was not a gentleman, Lillian," her mother hissed, adjusting the sleeves of her dress, and straightening her clothing. She appeared rather distressed, although Lillian could not imagine why. She had not seen her mother act in such a way before, and it puzzled her immensely.

"Mother, are you well?"

Lady Welsford narrowed her eyes at Lillian for a few moments and shook her head. She stared out of the window of the carriage and sighed theatrically.

"I hope you realize that everything I have done for you your entire life was to ensure that you were raised as a proper young woman who would easily find a husband."

"I do realize that. But you still have not answered my question. Are you well?"

"I am well. Your concern is appreciated, my dear. And I must apologize for my behavior. That gentleman outside the modiste was not the kind of man you should keep company with."

Lillian's brow furrowed, and her heart suddenly raced in her chest. Her palms felt clammy, and her cheeks colored once more. She lowered her gaze, to hide her affliction from her mother. She certainly did not need her mother to notice the flush in her cheeks at only the mention of the handsome stranger who had rescued her from an embarrassing fall in the busiest street in Mayfair.

"I understand, Mother, as you were quite clear the

first time. What I do not understand is why you were so rude to that gentleman. Are you familiar with him?"

"I am familiar with his type," Lady Welsford scoffed and crossed her arms. "And I would very much appreciate it if you were to stay as far away from him, and men like him, as possible in future."

Lillian pursed her lips as she noticed the carriage continue past their home in Mayfair.

"Mother, where are we going?"

"We are meeting your brother at the tearooms."

"Why was I not informed of this?"

"I do not require your permission to make any decisions, especially not when they involve important matters. We are to discuss a possible marriage in the near future."

"Whose marriage?"

"Yours, my dear."

"I beg your pardon. I did not agree to anything, nor have I been made aware of such plans."

"Again, dearest, I do not need to ask your permission for everything, and as a matter of fact, I said a *possible* marriage."

Lillian's jaw clenched angrily, but she bit her tongue. It was a futile thing to argue with her mother regarding matters of marriage and betrothals. She was in charge of that, much to Lillian's dismay, and she would not allow her daughter to sully the family name.

Since her Come Out three years ago, Lillian had longed to meet someone who not only shared her interests but who was also handsome and interesting. Most importantly, she wished for a love match. Unfortunately, at the rate she was going, that would never happen. If she was forced to marry someone, it would have to be someone she could tolerate.

And none of her mother's choices seemed to fit any of those criteria.

Upon their arrival at the tearooms, Lady Welsford immediately noticed Timothy waiting for them at a table by the window. Timothy enjoyed watching people, almost studying them. That was why he read people so very well. He was also an excellent judge of character and Lady Welsford often relied on his opinion regarding members of the *ton*. He could often advise on who to trust, and who to stay far away from.

"Oh, good. You are here. I was afraid that we would have to wait for you. I am practically parched."

Timothy hastily ordered their tea and glanced at his mother.

"Is everything well, Mother? You seem rather..."

His voice trailed off as he silently searched for the right word, but Lillian interjected.

"Distressed."

Timothy's brow furrowed and he shook his head in disagreement.

"I would not have used such a harsh word, but there does seem to be something amiss."

"Mother was informing me that I should keep better company and not mingle with men who would ruin my reputation with their behavior."

Timothy stared at his mother in confusion and inquired, "What prompted this?"

"I tripped outside the modiste's, and a kind gentleman caught me before I fell."

Lady Welsford's jaw tightened.

"Perhaps in the future, you should be more careful and mindful."

Lillian rolled her eyes and turned to her brother.

"He was lovely, Timothy. He was kind and handsome-"

"And not a good fit at all. Lord Bertram is a much better match."

"Lord Bertram? Are you seriously considering him as a suitable husband for Lillian?" Timothy asked.

"I am. His father was well-respected-"

"That does not mean that he is, Mother."

Lillian stared at her brother and mother, who were practically arguing about whether Lord Bertram was the kind of man Lillian should marry. Her mother was very happy with the idea, but her brother appeared very apprehensive. It was as though he knew something about Lord Bertram that their mother did not, and he was attempting to keep it concealed. Lillian found that rather surprising, as Timothy could persuade his mother of most things.

Unfortunately, when it came to Lord Bertram, her mother was steadfast and unmoving. She appeared to have made up her mind about Lillian marrying Lord Bertram. Perhaps Lillian must investigate on her own, and find out as much as she could about Lord Bertram.

But the only person on Lillian's mind was the handsome man who had caught her in front of the modiste. She still smelled the scent of him on her clothing and she would never be able to forget the intensity of his hazel eyes. Lillian shivered at the thought, and she lowered her gaze.

"But who was this stranger who rescued you from humiliation, sister?"

Timothy's voice startled her, and her thoughts of the handsome gentleman instantly vanished. She lightly shrugged her shoulders and sipped her tea.

"I am not certain. He was not able to introduce himself, nor was I for that matter."

"That is a pity, as it is clear that he made quite an impression on you, sister."

"What do you mean?"

"I have not seen your cheeks so colored in a long time, and you are smiling rather dreamily."

"Stop it," Lillian giggled.

"Perhaps you shall fall at his feet again and he will properly introduce himself."

"Or perhaps she ought to forget about a man who does not make an effort to introduce himself. The man is hiding something," Lade Welsford muttered before sipping her tea.

"The only reason he did not, was because you rudely interrupted him," Lillian pointed out.

"Is this true, Mother?"

"Please, spare me the interrogation. A man like that should not be walking the streets of Mayfair, not even during the off-season."

"I do not understand what this man did that made you despise him so," Lillian uttered.

"It does not matter, and *he* most certainly does not

matter. Shall we speak of Lord Bertram? It will be a much more pleasant conversation," Lady Welsford suggested.

"And what do you wish to discuss about Lord Bertram?" Timothy asked.

"I am arranging for him to call at our home in a few days. Perhaps we can invite him to have dinner with us as well. I do feel that he is a good match."

"He has shown an interest?"

"He has. In fact, he seems very interested."

"Really?" Lillian asked calmly.

"Indeed. Is that not wonderful? He owns a lovely country home in Kent and a townhouse in Grosvenor Square. Lillian would not be too far away. We could visit as often as they allow us, and you and Lord Bertram can get reacquainted."

"Reacquainted?"

"Lord Bertram attended Oxford with Timothy."

Lillian's eyes widened and she stared at her brother.

"You did not tell me this."

"I did not feel the need to. I wish you to make up your own mind about him, sister."

"Since when do I have that luxury?" Lillian muttered and rose to her feet. "Pardon me, I need some air."

Before Timothy and Lady Welsford were able to say anything, Lillian left the tearoom and stood outside. She drew in deep breaths and calmed herself. She was growing weary of her mother controlling her life, especially when it came to suitors.

Lillian looked around her, hoping to see the handsome gentleman she was not able to stop thinking of. Of course, she realized it was foolish, and wishful thinking from her side to even consider the possibility that he might wish to see her again. But there was no harm in looking around, after all, what were the chances that she would bump into him twice in a row?

"She is only taking care of you, Lillian," Timothy said, suddenly beside her.

Lillian gasped in surprise and turned to her brother.

"I hardly think that is true. She is determined to make my life miserable and marry me off to the man she wants me to marry. I have no say in it whatsoever."

Timothy shifted his weight from side to side and grinned at her.

"Perhaps you ought to show some interest in another suitor. Perhaps if you do that, she will not be as adamant."

"That would work, except that I have not met someone who has caught my interest, brother."

"What of this gentleman who caught you and stopped you from falling on your delicate little face?"

Lillian chuckled and her cheeks colored.

"I wish I knew his name. You would be able to find him with a snap of your fingers."

"You deem me very resourceful, sister."

Lillian playfully nudged Timothy and giggled.

"You are."

"I am," he admitted with amusement. "Please do not be hard on Mother. She is doing the best that she can."

Lillian sighed and tilted her head to the side.

"It is at times such as these that I wish I had a sister."

"We both know that would not help in the least,"

Timothy laughed. "But do not fret, sister. I am always here when you need me."

"Thank you, brother. I would not have been able to last as long as I have with Mother if it were not for you."

"Shall we go back inside, then? We should not leave Mother to her own devices, should we?"

Lillian grinned.

"Perhaps a few more minutes?"

"Very well."

Lillian smiled at her brother. Ever since she could remember, he had protected her, and shielded her from the dangers of the world, their mother included. And it was true what she had told him. If it was not for him, she would not have held out that long with her mother and her overbearing nature.

CHAPTER SEVEN

"There is the Duke."

With every step that Samuel took around Mayfair, members of the *ton* whispered not so subtly as he passed by. It was becoming very much an annoyance to him, and ignoring them was not an option any longer.

Rather than direct his anger at them, he restrained himself and made a clever decision. He knew that the newspaper the article was published in was printed by a printing shop in Lambeth, as he had visited the shop often as a child. His father had used the printers for his business purposes, but Samuel had not been there in many years. Nevertheless, he still remembered where it was located, and ordered his coachman to steer the carriage in that direction.

From inside the carriage, he watched as the streets of London passed him by. As they traveled to a different part of town, the view from his window changed rather suddenly, as soon as the carriage crossed Lambeth Bridge.

He was no longer in the upper-class part of town, and while Lambeth was perfectly respectable for him, as a gentleman, to stroll around in, it was certainly not a place for young women.

A smile appeared on Samuel's face as he thought of the young woman with the golden hair who he had saved from falling in Mayfair. The young lady had certainly made an impression on him, and he was unable to get her out of his mind. He was not certain how he would find her again, although he found that he wished to, but he had enough to deal with at present, and could not search for a golden-haired young lady as well as for the writer of the article.

Perhaps he should consider staying in London longer.

Once the carriage came to a halt, Samuel stepped down and inhaled sharply of the cold air. According to his knowledge, the printers were only a short distance from where his carriage had stopped, and he could walk the rest of the way.

"I will not be long," he said to his coachman, who nodded in response.

Samuel walked quietly along the cobblestones, finding the narrow street which he recalled walking along, beside his father. His mother was never too pleased when Samuel had accompanied his late father to the printers, as she claimed that it was not the place for an impressionable young boy such as him. But Samuel had never been impressionable. He had strict morals which he complied with, and he was a more than upstanding gentleman, which made it very strange that the *ton* believed the lies which had been written of him. Clearly, the *ton* did not know him very well, or, perhaps, it was simply that they would believe anything that was written in the newspapers. If they had spent a day in his company, they would realize that what had been written about him was absolute lies.

As he turned the corner, the printers' shop came into view, and luckily the doors were still open. A young man carried crates of papers into the shop, and Samuel quickened his step.

"Pardon me," he called out.

"Can I help you, sir?"

Although the young man had not correctly addressed him, Samuel did not correct him. In fact, it was better that Samuel's identity was not known to this man.

"I wish to make an inquiry."

"Of what?"

"An article was published in your newspaper two fortnights ago, and I wish to know who the author was."

"Follow me, sir."

Samuel briefly eyed his surroundings before he nodded at the young man and followed him into the printing shop. Boxes and stacks of newspapers were randomly positioned on the floor and the counter and the candles flickered on the table nearby. The young man approached an older balding man with a stout build and a shirt that was much too tight.

"Good afternoon, sir. I am Mr. Charles Hunter, the owner of Lambeth Printers. How can I assist you today?" the man said to Samuel.

"It is a pleasure to meet you, Mr. Hunter. As I mentioned to this young man, an article was published in your newspaper. Is there any possibility of knowing who the writer was?"

"When was this?"

"It was two fortnights ago," Samuel said and retrieved the article that Timothy had sent him from his breast pocket.

He handed the article to Mr. Hunter who adjusted his glasses on the bridge of his wide nose.

"Hm, I remember this. I was surprised that someone would write such things about a Duke. I've never personally heard of the man, but what was written was terrible."

Samuel's jaw clenched, and he nodded.

"It is enough to ruin his fine reputation. You do not perhaps remember the man who delivered the article to be published?"

"Let me check my books. The transaction must be noted. We do that for private articles."

"That would be of great assistance. Thank you, sir."

Samuel watched as Mr. Hunter rummaged around in the drawer in front of him and retrieved a thick book. He paged through the book rather roughly, scanning down the list of names written in it with ink-stained fingers.

"What was the date on the newspaper it was published in?

"November nine-and-tenth," Samuel answered.

Mr. Hunter nodded and studied the book again.

"The only entry I have is on the previous day. John Smith."

Samuel's lips pursed and his jaw clenched. Unfortunately, that name did not mean much to him. It could be anyone since it was a very common name, which did not help Samuel a great deal. It was certainly not what he had expected to find.

"Do you recall anything about him? Anything significant?"

"I do not recall his face. He must have been particularly bland. But I did note in the book that he was full of juice."

"And why do you say that?" Samuel inquired.

"He paid much more than our usual rate. Triple the amount, for that matter. He wanted to make sure that the article was published, I suppose."

"He certainly did."

Samuel was rather irate that his journey to Lambeth had turned out to be such a fruitless endeavor. He had hoped that he could track down the person who had provided the article to be published, or at least find out what that person's name was. But he had underestimated the writer of the article. He had used a name that was so common that there was no way to identify him accurately. It also might not have been the writer himself who had visited the printers. Perhaps he had paid someone to take the article to the printers and given him more than enough coin to compensate for the inconvenience and the short notice.

"I am sorry that I cannot be of more help, sir."

Mr. Hunter handed the article back to Samuel and Samuel placed the folded paper back into his pocket.

"Do you perhaps have the original article?"

"Unfortunately, we do not keep the original writings for more than a fortnight, sir."

Samuel lowered his gaze for a moment and balled his fists. Every idea that he had was immediately terminated by Mr. Hunter, and it was utterly frustrating. His questions were not being answered the way he wanted them to be, and he was running out of options.

How was he supposed to catch this person?

"Thank you, Mr. Hunter. I appreciate the information."

Samuel turned on his heel and hastily left the printers, grumbling to himself. He had hoped that he would find out more about the writer, but the only thing that he had learned was that the person was fairly flush in the pockets. But, of course, that did not narrow it down, as many wealthy people in London could have funded this.

Samuel walked briskly along the cobblestone streets back to his carriage, his mind in a befogged state. He was beginning to be angered by the unanswered questions that tumbled through his thoughts, and he was not certain what to do. There was no way of knowing who the writer was, and he felt rather annoyed.

"Yarmouth?"

Samuel spun around in surprise and was relieved to see Lord Timothy standing beside his carriage. He certainly did not need anyone to see him in Lambeth, especially not given the circumstances. Behind Lord Timothy, the Colborne family carriage stood, and he breathed a sigh of relief.

"Colborne," Samuel nodded and approached his friend.

"What on earth are you doing this side of the Thames?" Lord Timothy asked.

"I visited the printers of the newspaper in an attempt to find the person who wrote the article, or at least to find the person who handed the article to the printers to be published."

"And?" Lord Timothy asked apprehensively.

"Nothing. All the man was able to tell me was that the man was fairly flush in the pockets."

Lord Timothy shifted his weight from one foot to the other.

"But that could be anyone."

"I realize that."

"That is a pity."

"Indeed. But I am determined not to give up. I cannot allow this man to ruin my reputation the way that he is," Samuel said and drew in a deep breath.

"But how will you find him?"

"I am not certain. I am, however, growing increasingly agitated by this. What gives this man the right to drag my name through the mud for his enjoyment? How dare he think that he can get away with this?"

Lord Timothy placed his hand on Samuel's shoulder and slowly uttered, "Calm yourself, my friend. We will find out who did this, I promise you that."

"You will assist me?"

"Indeed I will, but you must remain calm. There is no point in you upsetting yourself."

Samuel pursed his lips and turned to Timothy.

"What would you suggest we do?"

"First of all, we need to get you back to Mayfair. This

is certainly not the sort of place you wish to be seen, given the rumors that are spreading through Town of your supposed indiscretions."

"Although they are untrue," Samuel muttered, but it was of no use.

People would think of him what they wished, and there was nothing he could do about it. Finding the person responsible was the only way to restore his reputation.

Lord Timothy patted his shoulder reassuringly.

"We will restore your reputation and find the person responsible for those rumors."

"Thank you, Colborne. What *are* you doing here, if I may ask?"

"I was looking for you, of course. Your housekeeper said you took the carriage, and I realized that you must be on the hunt."

On the hunt, Samuel thought with bland amusement.

"Not a very successful hunt, I might add."

"Perhaps you need some distraction," Lord Timothy said.

"What do you suggest?" Samuel asked.

"Have dinner with me and my family this evening. It would be delightful having you at Welsford House."

"And what of your mother? Surely she is aware of the rumors of me."

Timothy smiled with reassurance.

"Do not fret. I have already mentioned it to my mother, and she agreed."

"Are you certain? I do not wish to upset your mother

or your family. I also do not wish to harm your family's good name with my sordid reputation," Samuel sighed and stepped back.

"You and I both know that the rumors are not true and, once my family meets you, they will know it as well. After all, my parents haven't seen you since that one time shortly after we finished at Oxford."

"Regardless, my presence will only-"

"I will not take no for an answer," Lord Timothy interjected. "It would be an honor to have you join us for dinner. You can even meet my sister."

Samuel was surprised at this new information.

"You have a sister, Colborne?"

"Indeed, I do."

"Is she as outspoken and persistent as you are?" Samuel asked jokingly.

"Even more so."

The Duke chuckled and finally gave in to his friend.

"I would love to join you and your family for dinner."

Lord Timothy smiled happily at him, but Samuel could not help but feel tense at the thought of the rumors about him that would potentially cause harm to the Colborne family. He was the brother he'd never had, and he would not forgive himself if he ruined their reputations. Lord Timothy had been nothing but accommodating and kind to Samuel and the best friend he could have asked for. Despite not spending as much time with one another as Samuel would have liked, their letters to one another in Samuel 's absence had managed to close the gap between the two friends. And the moment that

Samuel had set foot in London, their friendship had resumed as if no time had passed.

Admittedly, Samuel was nervous about meeting Lord Timothy's family, not knowing how they would react if they were to see him, but he did look forward to meeting Timothy's sister.

CHAPTER EIGHT

"Timothy, I do not even know what to say."

Lillian was on her way to the drawing room, clutching a new book that her father had gifted to her when she overheard her mother hissing those words. She stopped abruptly in her tracks and pursed her lips. The sound came from inside the study, and the door was only slightly ajar. Not enough for Lillian to see inside, but she could hear the conversation well enough.

Timothy had invited a guest to dinner that evening, as he had announced a few days earlier, and clearly, Lady Welsford was not pleased about it. She had been in a foul mood ever since she'd been told of it. It started to make sense to Lillian now as she listened. She came to the conclusion that this irritated mood was the reason her mother had been so incredibly rude to the gentleman outside the modiste.

"When you informed me that you had invited a guest for dinner, and to spend Christmas with us, I never dreamed that it would be him."

"But Mother, why on earth should it matter? He *is* a good friend and, since his mother passed away, he does not have any family left."

"I am certain it is not such a tragedy as you make it out to be, my darling," Lord Welsford pointed out.

"Indeed it is. What if people were to find out that he is here? What would that do to our reputation?"

"Mother, you are exaggerating."

"I most certainly am not. That man-"

"That man is my friend, and I will not allow you to speak of him in such a manner."

Lillian's brow furrowed and she stood closer to the door. Were they speaking of the Duke of Yarmouth? Had Timothy invited *the* Duke of Yarmouth to their family dinner?

"Have you read what was written about him? He gambled away his fortune, which now has him in financial ruin, not even to mention the haunts that he frequents. I will not allow anyone to disgrace this family. We certainly do not need a scandal on our hands."

"Mother-"

"Is it not enough that neither you nor your sister are yet married, and I am still without a grandchild? Must you torture me by bringing into my home a man who does not have even a shred of decency in his body?"

Lillian's brow furrowed and she stepped away angrily. She knew that her mother was upset that she had not found a husband yet, but Lillian had not realized that her mother was ashamed of this. It shocked her that her mother was disappointed and felt ashamed that her adult children had not married. That was the very first time that Lillian had heard her express any anger and shame towards Timothy about not being married yet. She had always felt that her mother placed pressure upon her to marry, and not on Timothy. But it seemed that their mother was equally ashamed of both of her children.

Not wishing to upset herself any further, Lillian stepped away from the door of the study and quietly made her way downstairs. The drawing room had always been her favorite room to unwind and clear her head. Since it was a quiet room as well, she did most of her reading there. In contrast, it was also the place where she met countless callers who expressed an interest in courting her. Although she had not received a single proposal from those suitors who had called, she realized that perhaps it was time to set her pride aside and give such things a chance.

Perhaps Lord Bertram was not as bad a choice for a husband as she thought. He was certainly a handsome gentleman, with deep brown eyes and a quirky smile which gave Lillian rather mixed feelings. He was well-spoken and had impeccable manners. But he did not make her skin tingle or cause her heart to race as the gentleman in front of the modiste had.

Lillian had to accept that, quite possibly, no other man would have such an effect on her.

If only she knew his name.

But what use would it be? After the way that her mother had glared at the man, he had most certainly been instantly put off by her behavior, and would not make any attempt to find out who she was.

Lillian sighed as she stepped into the drawing room,

and found her usual reading spot waiting for her. It was a chaise placed in a secluded corner, hidden away from initial sight. She sat on the chaise, made herself comfortable, and began to read. She soon became so immersed in the pages of her new book that she did not even notice the footsteps approaching the drawing room. Or the person who entered.

"Oh, pardon me. I was not aware that someone was here," he apologized.

Lillian instantly recognized the baritone voice, and her head snapped up. She gasped quite loudly and rose to her feet. Placing her book down on the chaise, she subtly tidied her hair. She could not believe her eyes and blinked numerous times to ensure that she was not seeing things that were not there.

The gentleman was equally stunned as he stared at her. The same hazel eyes that pierced her being and made her heart race were now looking at her with both shock and relief.

"It is you," he uttered, his voice as smooth and luxurious as velvet.

"Me? I mean, indeed. And it is you, my savior from outside the modiste's."

"I would hardly refer to myself in such a way. I simply did what any gentleman would do for a beautiful young lady in distress."

"You think that I am beautiful?" she asked, unable to contain herself.

"Strikingly so."

Lillian gasped softly and subtly smoothed out the folds of her pale blue dress. It was one of her favorites, with matching lace trim wrapped around the bodice and the long sleeves.

"How did you find me?" she asked.

"I can ask you the same question."

"I did not find you. I live here."

The gentleman's eyes widened in shock, and he glanced around the room. "You live *here*? In this very house?"

Lillian cocked her head and stared at him in confusion.

"Indeed. You appear surprised."

"I am. I did not expect to see you here. You are Lord Timothy Colborne's sister?"

"I am. How did you know?"

"I have known your brother since our days at Oxford. He is a very good friend of mine."

Lillian's eyes widened once more, and she stared at him in disbelief.

Never in her life could she have expected that the handsome young man who had come to her aid would be the same man who had been friends with her brother at Oxford. Why had she not heard of him, or seen him, before?

Timothy had attended Oxford over seven years ago, and not once had she been introduced to, or seen, his very close friend.

And why would her mother be so unkind and upset over his presence?

Lillian was rather confused by this and felt as if she did not understand anything anymore. Perhaps she should mind her own business, and stop eavesdropping on her mother's conversations.

But how else would she know what went on between the walls of Welsford House? Her mother did not allow her to speak freely, nor did she ever engage Lillian in the adult conversations between her mother and father. It was as though her mother shielded her from everything that was not rose-colored and proper.

Frankly, Lillian was fed up with not being included in anything important - she was not included in decision-making, or choosing who would be a suitable husband for her.

"I apologize. I was not aware of this."

The gentleman stepped closer to her, and immediately, her heart pounded in her chest, and she felt her cheeks flush. His gaze grew intense, his eyes darkening, and his jaw eased. He was much taller than she was, his shoulders broad, and his intoxicating scent filled her nostrils. It reminded her of how she'd felt when he caught her, his strong arms wrapped around her waist, shielding her from hitting the ground in front of her.

She no longer felt embarrassed but was disappointed in herself that she had not asked for his name that day. If she'd known who he was, she would have tracked him down much sooner. Perhaps she would have spoken to her mother about this gentleman and persuaded her that, out of all the suitors she had met, he was the one she wanted.

If he wanted to have her, of course, but the intensity of his gaze already proved that he did. At least she thought so.

"I wish to thank you for what you did for me. I was certain that I would die of embarrassment and never be able to show my face around town again if I had fallen. If it were not for you, I probably would have."

"And that would be a terrible fate indeed."

Lillian was on the verge of swooning over the gentleman and his smooth words that caressed her soul in all the right ways.

"And I must apologize for my mother's behavior. How she spoke to you was unacceptable. She is rather adamant in her pursuit of finding a suitor for me, and is extremely careful about my reputation."

"There is no need for you to apologize on her behalf. I am certain that she had her reasons. I will not hold it against her, or you." The gentleman shifted his weight and stared intently at Lillian. "And why is it that your mother wishes you to be married as soon as possible?"

Lillian tensed at his question.

"I'd rather not answer that."

As he was on the verge of responding, footsteps were heard in the hallway, growing louder by the second.

"Apologies for the wait, Yarmouth. I had to straighten out a misunderstanding..."

Timothy's voice trailed off as he entered the drawing room. He stopped abruptly as he noticed that Lillian was also present in the room. Under normal circumstances, it was not proper for a young, unmarried woman to be in the presence of a gentleman without a chaperone, but it was Lillian's home as well, and perhaps it could be overlooked – although really, she should have left the room the moment that he'd entered it, for propriety's sake.

"Ah, I see that you two have already met," Timothy said slowly.

Lillian immediately took a step back, as did the handsome gentleman, but it now felt as if he was much too far away from Lillian, much to her dismay.

"Indeed we have. I was not aware that you had such a beautiful sister, Colborne."

"Of course. It goes without saying that she's beautiful - simply take a look at my mother," Timothy grinned as Lady and Lord Welsford also entered the drawing room.

Lillian would have grown shy and her cheeks colored, but as she turned her attention to her mother, she was distracted by how pale her mother looked.

Her mother's eyes were narrowed, her lips pursed into a thin line and her shoulders were tense. She wore what could only be described as an expression of contempt and disdain as she glared at the gentleman in the drawing room.

"We have not been formally introduced yet, brother," Lillian pointed out to her brother.

A brilliant, yet somewhat tense smile appeared on her brother's face, his eyes sparkling with delight.

"Yarmouth, this is my lovely sister, Lady Lillian Colborne."

Lillian smiled at him with a nod.

"Sister, may I introduce my good friend, His Grace, the Duke of Yarmouth."

Lillian's smile immediately disappeared and was replaced by a look of shock and surprise, followed by a gasp. She had not expected that the man who had gallantly rescued her would turn out to be the Duke of

Yarmouth. He was the very man who she'd heard the two ladies speak of at the modiste. But how could that be true?

How could that delightfully polite and charming man be the same man who was said to have gambled away his fortune and who kept the company of women of easy virtue?

That was simply not possible. She could not believe it of him.

"It is a pleasure to make your acquaintance, Lady Lillian."

"And you, Your Grace."

Lillian smoothed her dress and glanced at her mother, who was still speechless. The color had returned to her face, and it was more prominent now than ever. It was quiet in the drawing room for what felt like an eternity until Lady Welsford cleared her throat and turned to Lord Welsford.

"If the *ton* were to hear of this-"

"That is quite enough, my dear," Lord Welsford interjected. "Now, shall we all go to the dining room? Dinner is served."

Lillian pursed her lips and, as they left the drawing room, she could not help but notice the Duke's gaze on her as she walked past him to the dining room.

CHAPTER NINE

Samuel was impressed with the dinner table and realized that the Colborne family was much wealthier than he had thought. He had known that Lord Timothy was the only son of the Earl of Welsford, who was a very influential man with numerous business dealings, but he had certainly underestimated their success.

Welsford House was an exquisite home in Mayfair, with stone steps that led to the front door, and lavender bushes with a delicate and delightful scent. The home was large in comparison to other houses in the street, which made the Colbornes' success and status obvious. Both the drawing room and the dining room in the home were spacious and luxuriously decorated, with furnishings that certainly appeared to be imported.

The drawing room, where he had laid eyes on Lady Lillian after believing that he would never see her again, was bright even during the sunset. The room was drenched in a golden glow, illuminating her skin, and he was both stunned and mesmerized by her beauty. Even during dinner, it was rather difficult for Samuel to tear his eyes away from her. Much to his delight, she spoke often, and it would have been considered rude if he did not look at her while she spoke.

"What brings you back to London, Your Grace?" Lord Welsford asked. "I understand that your estate is in Cornwall."

Samuel softly cleared his throat and looked at Lord Welsford.

"I have some business to tend to in town, my Lord."

"And it could not wait until after Christmas?" Lady Welsford asked, her eyes narrowed and sharply focused on Samuel.

"It was not something I could wave off until the new year, my Lady. It is quite urgent and requires my immediate attention."

"What kind of business, Your Grace?" Lady Lillian inquired, and Samuel gazed at her, his eyes softening.

"Darling, do not be intrusive," Lady Welsford warned her daughter.

"My apologies, Your Grace," Lady Lillian lowered her gaze.

"That is quite alright, Lady Lillian. And she was not being intrusive, my Lady."

"Father says that I have an inquisitive mind."

"The most inquisitive you will ever meet," Lord Welsford smiled.

Samuel nodded and Lady Lillian's eye met his briefly.

"It is a good trait to have."

Lady Lillian's cheeks colored, and her gaze lowered to her meal.

"The dinner is delicious," Samuel said quietly. "Please give my compliments to your cook, my Lady."

"I will do so, Your Grace."

"How is Cornwall this time of the year, Your Grace?" Lord Welsford inquired.

"Cold, dull, and wet, my Lord."

"Not much different than London, then?"

"I would rather experience a snowstorm in London than any winter's day in Cornwall. The cold is indescribable. It seeps into your bones, chilling your soul."

"I can only imagine how miserable that must be, especially after the tragic death of your mother, and so soon after your father's passing as well. Our sincerest condolences."

Samuel's jaw clenched slightly, and he nodded.

"Thank you, my Lord. It was quite a shock to the family."

"You live alone at your estate, Your Grace?" Lady Lillian asked.

"Indeed."

"Is it not terribly lonely?"

A morose smile appeared on his lips, and he nodded once more. The empathy in Lady Lillian's eyes was heartwarming and her kind heart was evident in the manner she looked at him.

"It can be, especially since your brother has failed to visit in the past two years."

Lord Timothy chuckled.

"I must apologize. I have been meaning to, I promise. But you have not come to London, either."

"Indeed - but time passes rather quickly when one is engaged in things that take precedence, and the management of the estate has been topmost since my father's sickness and passing."

"Truer words have never been spoken," Lord Welsford pointed out. "At times we do not realize how speedily time moves."

"Indeed, my Lord."

"Surely Your Grace does not need to stay in Cornwall all year round."

"I have considered occupying my townhouse in Mayfair, which I must admit would be much more convenient, but I have had estate matters to deal with," Samuel said.

"I am certain that Timothy would enjoy having Your Grace closer," Lady Lillian said, with a hint of a mischievous smile.

"Indeed, I would," Lord Timothy agreed.

Samuel grinned at Lady Lillian, and they shared a moment that made Samuel believe that she was not referring to her brother, but to herself, and he discovered that he felt the same, that he would not mind living closer to Lady Lillian.

"Your brother told me that you and he are much alike. Is that true?"

Lady Lillian tilted her head to the side and a lock of golden hair brushed her shoulder.

"I do not know what Your Grace means?"

"He mentioned that you are outspoken and persistent, even more so than he is."

"My brother flatters me, and he is not wrong. But unlike my brother, I enjoy reading."

Samuel smiled brightly.

"Delightful. What have you been reading of late?"

"I have been enjoying the works of Shakespeare, but my most recent book is a novel called Pride and Prejudice. It is rather good and very well written."

"That is an Austen novel, is it not?"

"Your Grace knows of her?"

"Indeed. My father had quite an extensive collection of books in his library, and after his passing, I took it upon myself to continue to grow his collection."

"Father has been allowing me to grow my collection in the upstairs drawing room. Perhaps after dinner, I can show Your Grace."

Lord Timothy scoffed.

"Dear Lillian. I am certain that the Duke does not want to see your silly little collection of novels."

"They are not silly. They are wonderful literary works."

"I would love to," Samuel said, much to everyone's surprise.

"Perhaps not," Lady Welsford said firmly. "It is already enough that His Grace was invited for dinner. I cannot allow you to be in the upstairs drawing room without a chaperone."

"Mother-"

"It is settled, Lillian."

Lady Lillian nodded and lowered her gaze. Her mother's firm response was somewhat unfair, but Samuel understood that Lady Welsford did not wish her daughter to be alone with him, especially because of the rumors around Town.

Throughout dinner Samuel listened to Lord Welsford and Lord Timothy as they engaged in conversation with him, responding appropriately. The ladies at the table did not speak much, apart from Lady Welsford's occasional comment. Lady Lillian kept mostly to herself, although Samuel could see that she had many things on her mind. He certainly hoped that he was one of those things.

"How long will you be staying in town?" Lord Welsford asked.

"Well, Lord Timothy invited me to spend Christmas with your family, and I believe that I shall return to Cornwall in the new year. Perhaps even sooner if my business here is concluded," Samuel answered.

"Your Grace, may I ask a question?" Lady Lillian asked suddenly.

"Lillian, I am certain that His Grace does not wish to be bombarded with questions," her mother warned.

Samuel raised his hand calmly.

"It is alright, my Lady." He turned to Lady Lillian and nodded. "Of course, Lady Lillian."

"Is Your Grace's visit to Town due to my brother's invitation solely, or does it have anything to do with the rumors about Your Grace?" Lady Lillian inquired, astonishing both her parents and her brother.

"Lillian," Lady Welsford warned. "This is not a suitable topic of conversation. It is quite improper, so I would appreciate it if you were to stop, right this instant."

"That is quite alright, my Lady," Samuel dismissed her concerns. "I am certain that Lady Lillian did not mean any offense."

"I did not, Your Grace. I did not mean to show any disrespect," Lady Lillian spoke slowly, her eyes sparkling.

"There is no need to apologize. But while we are on the subject, allow me to clear the air. Indeed, there are rumors around town of me."

"Which are completely false," Lord Timothy stated clearly. "His Grace has not even been in London for the last two years, to do what is said of him."

Lady Welsford appeared unconvinced by this and raised an apprehensive brow.

"If the claims are false, why is everyone speaking of it?"

Samuel hesitated and glanced at Lord Timothy, who appeared ready to answer any questions.

"It appears that someone falsely wrote those tales of His Grace to ruin his reputation on purpose," Lord Timothy answered. "It was published in the Lambeth Times, and it spread like wildfire. His Grace does not deserve to be shunned from society because of untruths."

Lady Lillian frowned and shook her head.

"But who would do such a thing? From what I have seen tonight, Your Grace is not worthy to be shunned."

"Thank you, Lady Lillian. Your words are kind. To answer your question, I am not certain," Samuel answered, and their gazes locked for a short time. "I was hoping that my return to Town would enable me to seek out the person, but I am not certain whether it will be possible to locate him."

"And what makes Your Grace think it is a man?" Lady Lillian asked quietly.

Samuel's brow furrowed, and he stared at Lady Lillian with a puzzled expression.

"That is a rather good question," Lord Welsford pointed out. "Are there any suspects?"

Lady Welsford placed her cutlery on her plate loudly, the clattering echoed through the dining room.

"You all speak as though this is a mystery that needs to be solved."

"But it is, Mother."

"And it is quite intriguing, you must admit, darling."

"No, it is not. I have expressed my feelings towards His Grace rather forthrightly and I stand by it. I do not wish our family's reputation to be sullied by these rumors as a result of Timothy insisting on inviting the Duke to join us for dinner and Christmas. And although I will not chase His Grace from our home, please do not expect me to be happy with this arrangement. Come along, Lillian. Let us allow the gentlemen to speak freely amongst themselves. Their discussions are certainly not for our delicate ears."

"But I have not finished."

"*Now*, Lillian."

Lady Welsford rose to her feet and stared expectantly at Lady Lillian. Lady Lillian placed her cutlery on her plate and slowly rose to her feet with a sigh.

"It was lovely to meet you, Your Grace," she said quietly.

"And you, Lady Lillian."

As the two ladies left the dining room, the gentlemen were quiet as the tension lingered for a few moments.

Lord Welsford wiped the corner of his mouth and looked at Samuel.

"I apologize for my wife. She is rather stressed at the moment. It is Lillian's third Season since her Come Out and she has not yet found a suitable match. It has taken its toll on my wife."

"And what of Lady Lillian?"

"Whatever do you mean?"

"Has searching for a husband taken its toll on your daughter as well?"

Lord Timothy chuckled.

"She seems rather uninterested in the idea of marriage. Why do you ask? Are you interested, Yarmouth?"

Samuel laughed in amusement but felt oddly nervous at the question.

"Of course not. That would mean I would be related to you."

"Only by marriage, luckily."

They laughed, then turned their attention to other things, relaxing into convivial conversation.

As the evening drew to a close, Samuel thanked Lord Welsford for his hospitality. Soon after, Lord Timothy saw Samuel out, and, whilst he had hoped that he would have the opportunity to say good night to Lady Lillian, she was nowhere in sight. He also did not wish to ask, as Lord Timothy would tease him relentlessly if he thought Samuel to be truly interested in his sister. He certainly did not need that from his friend.

The two gentlemen stepped outside. Stars sparkled overhead, the winter evening air was cold, and a chill ran down Samuel's spine.

"Thank you for a very spirited and eventful evening, Colborne."

"I am glad that you enjoyed it - apart from my mother making a scene, I thought it was rather successful," Timothy grinned.

"Please apologize to your mother for me if I have offended her in any way."

Lord Timothy scoffed.

"Do not mind my mother. She concerns herself with things she ought not to."

Samuel nodded.

"Good night, Colborne."

"Good night, Yarmouth."

Samuel climbed into his carriage and watched Lord Timothy return to Welsford House. Right before the carriage pulled away, Samuel turned his gaze upward and noticed an illuminated window on the second floor. Lady Lillian stood by the window, her golden hair tumbling down over her shoulders, and she stared at him for a moment. A moment that seemed to last an impossible length of time, as he was taken by her beauty and the way that she gazed at him. A grin appeared on Samuel's lips and as the carriage pulled away, his heart pounded in his chest.

Despite not having had the opportunity to bid the lovely young lady a good night, seeing her looking down at him was more than enough for Samuel.

CHAPTER TEN

Lillian stared at the nearly empty cup of tea on the table before her, her appetite dwindling. Her thoughts remained on last night when she had stood at her window and watched the Duke as he stepped up into his carriage. He had noticed her at her window, and they shared a moment filled with tension and exhilaration. Never in her life had Lillian felt emotions quite as strongly as she did for the Duke of Yarmouth. She was well aware of the rumors about the Duke, but not certain whether she believed them to be true. Timothy had made it clear during dinner that they were mere rumors made up by an unknown person, but her mother seemed convinced that they were true.

"You are awfully quiet this morning, sister."

Timothy's words brought Lillian back to the present moment and she shifted her gaze to her brother.

They were seated at the breakfast table, the rain clattering against the windows, and there was a chill in the air. Lillian was certain that it was the aftermath of the terrible evening they had experienced. She had desperately wished to stay at the dinner table, but her mother had not allowed her to. It was frustrating and reminded her that she would never have control of her life. Perhaps marriage was the escape she needed from her mother's controlling ways.

"Usually, you would be talking non-stop."

Lillian shrugged her shoulders gently and sighed.

"What did you, Father, and the Duke speak of, after I was so forcefully removed from the dining room?"

Timothy shook his head.

"Our conversation is not for such delicate ears as yours, Lillian."

"Please, Timothy?"

"I cannot, even if I wanted to."

"That is not fair," she muttered.

"Do not fret. There is nothing to worry about."

Lillian shook her head.

"I am not worried. I am curious."

"Curious about what?"

"Did the Duke do those things that were printed about him in the newspaper?" she asked.

"Of course he did not."

Lillian's brow furrowed and she rested her hands on her lap.

"How can you be certain?"

"Lillian, I have known him for a long time, and he is not the type of man who would do such things. He is a good man and a good friend. He would not lie to me."

"Everyone tells lies."

"And you have experience in this?" Timothy asked.

"You lied to Mother by not telling her that you had invited the Duke."

"I did not lie. I merely answered vaguely."

"A lie of omission is still a lie, Timothy," Lillian pointed out. "You were fully aware of Mother's probable reaction if she found out that you had invited the Duke to spend Christmas with us."

"I apologize. Is that what you wish me to say?"

Lillian sipped her tea and set her cup down on the table.

"I wish you to tell me the truth."

"I will not disclose what we spoke of at dinner, sister."

Lillian shook her head and cleared her throat.

"That is not what I mean. I wish for the truth. Did the Duke do all of those things?"

Timothy turned to Lillian and looked directly at her.

"I swear to you, Lillian. Yarmouth did not do those things. And how could he? He has been in Cornwall for two years. He has not even set foot in London in that time."

"And you are certain of this?"

"He and I have been corresponding since he returned to Cornwall. Each week I would receive a letter from him and write one in return. There is no possible way that he was anywhere close to London."

"He did not gamble himself into financial ruin?"

"He did not."

"And he did not visit undesirable haunts?"

"Not at all. The Duke is a man of integrity and

morals. He may visit Brooks with me, but his only vice is his tenacity," Timothy answered.

"Why is he in London, apart from joining us for Christmas?" Lillian asked.

"He is determined to find the writer of the article and restore his reputation."

Lillian tilted her head to the side, studying her brother's face. She had always been able to tell when her brother did not speak the truth, and today, she was certain that everything he had just said to her about the Duke and the false rumors was the truth.

It was quite a relief to know that. She did not wish to have feelings for a man who had gambled away his fortune and visited places that any respectable man did not set foot inside. She did not even wish to think of it, but Timothy's confirmation of his innocence certainly eased her worries.

"And how would he do that?" Lillian inquired as she crinkled her nose.

"He visited the printers of the newspaper to see if they could give him any information about the man who brought the article into the printers to be published. But unfortunately, that enquiry yielded little in the way of results."

"He found out nothing?"

"Only that the person paid triple the normal rate, in coin."

Lillian's brow furrowed and her lips pursed momentarily.

"A wealthy member of the *ton* is not very much to go on, Timothy."

"Indeed."

She stared at her empty cup of tea and her shoulders straightened.

"I would very much like to help."

"Help with what?"

"With finding the person responsible."

Timothy nearly choked on his tea and looked at Lillian in shock and surprise.

"That is preposterous."

"Why? I can be resourceful if given the chance," Lillian grinned and raised her chin, her lashes fluttering.

"I do not doubt that for a moment, sister, but Mother will never allow you to do that. She is far too set on finding you a husband."

"Lord Bertram, I assume. She has been speaking of him non-stop. It is rather annoying," Lillian sighed and rolled her eyes.

"Lord Bertram? She honestly thinks that *he* is the best suitor for you?" Timothy uttered in disgust.

"Indeed."

"I can now understand your defiance."

Lillian narrowed her eyes and wondered what Timothy was not telling her about Lord Bertram. At the mere mention of his name, each time, Timothy's jaw tightened, and his eyes were dark with animosity.

"What is it about Lord Bertram that you do not like, brother?"

Timothy shifted in his seat and his jaw tightened in its usual manner when the subject was brought up. He straightened his waistcoat and softly cleared his throat, attempting to appear nonchalant.

He failed miserably.

"He is not the right suitor for you."

Lillian rested her elbow on the table and her chin on her hand. Usually, her mother would not allow her to rest her elbows on the table, since that was not what a proper lady did.

"And since when has that become a concern of yours? I was convinced that you and Mother were trying to marry me off to the first gentleman who came calling."

"That is not true. I have always had your best interests at heart. But I must disagree with Mother. Lord Bertram is not a suitable husband for you. For another young lady, perhaps. But not for you."

Timothy had been a protective older brother since Lillian could remember, but never before to this degree. There was definitely something Timothy was not telling her.

"Lord Bertram also attended Oxford. Do you know him from there? Were you friends?"

"No, we were most certainly not friends. And why do you have all these questions?" Timothy asked with clear discomfort.

"I only wish to know why you think that he is not a good suitor."

"You will not have a fulfilled life with him, Lillian, and that is all I will say on the matter," Timothy said.

Lillian studied him for a moment, hoping he would change his mind and tell her what he knew, but much to her dismay, he did not.

At this rate, she might never know.

"Timothy, I-"

"Lillian, darling," Lady Welsford entered the room theatrically, a bright smile on her face.

Lillian turned away from Timothy and hastily removed her elbow from the table before her mother saw it. But she did not appear to notice anything, especially not the guilty expression on Lillian's face, or the annoyed expression on Timothy's.

"Mother, you are in a cheerful mood this morning," Timothy said as he rose to his feet.

"I am indeed. There is a gentleman caller for you this morning, Lillian."

Lillian's shoulders tensed and she gazed at her mother.

"Who is it, Mother?"

"Lord Bertram," Lady Welsford beamed and clasped her hands together. "Isn't that delightful?"

"Very much so, Mother."

"Come along then, Lillian. Let us not keep the gentleman waiting."

Lillian bit her lower lip and sighed. She rose from the table and smoothed the skirt of her pale green day dress.

"Let us not."

Lillian followed her mother into the drawing room, and the memory of the Duke flashed before her. The Duke was incredibly handsome, and yesterday he had been dressed in formal attire with an air of sophistication surrounding him. His dark brown hair had been meticulously styled and Lillian's skin tingled from the memory.

As she stepped inside, Lord Bertram turned from where he stood at the window.

"Lady Lillian," he beamed, his eyes intently focused on her.

"My Lord, how lovely it is to see you."

"You look radiant this morning, I must say. "

Lillian nodded tightly, forcing a smile.

"You are too kind, my Lord. Shall we sit?"

Lord Bertram motioned to the sofa, and they sat on opposite ends. Lady Welsford lingered in the background, and Lillian was rather grateful. She did not wish to be alone with Lord Bertram, especially since Timothy knew something about him that he did not want to disclose to Lillian.

"I brought you a gift, Lady Lillian."

"You did not need to do that, my Lord, Indeed, that is a little... presumptuous of you..." she insisted.

Behind her, she heard a small rustle which indicated that her mother had just stiffened, not entirely happy that Lord Bertram had done something that wasn't quite proper.

"I wanted to, Lady Lillian. When I saw it, I knew that I had to get it for you."

Much to Lillian's surprise, Lord Bertram revealed a small wooden carved box and handed it to her. It was not very heavy, and Lillian's curiosity was too much to contain. She lifted the lid and stared at a lovely brooch of a dragonfly, with a green gemstone set in the center of its body.

She gasped softly and lightly fingered the delicate brooch.

"It is beautiful. I have never seen anything like it. Thank you, my Lord. But what prompted this gift?"

"When your mother invited me to Welsford House, I was relieved, and delighted of course. I did not think that I would ever have the opportunity to call upon you, Lady Lillian."

"My mother speaks of you a lot, so it does not surprise me that she invited you, my Lord," Lillian pointed out.

"That is certainly a relief to hear. She appears to be more fond of me than your brother is."

"I do not understand it either. Were you and Timothy not at Oxford together?" Lillian asked. "I asked him, and it seems that he does not wish to give me a straight answer. I do not know why."

"Simply because we attended the same university does not make us friends. Perhaps your brother is protective of his sister, and only wishes the best for you."

"I am not certain of anything any longer," Lillian said and gazed at the brooch. "Thank you for the lovely gift, my Lord. It is truly beautiful."

"Not nearly as beautiful as you, Lady Lillian."

Lillian lowered her gaze shyly and her cheek colored. It was not every day that she was called beautiful by a prospective suitor, much less one sitting on the other side of the sofa with her.

"You are too kind with your words."

"Lady Lillian, I believe that Lady Montague is hosting a festive ball the evening after tomorrow. If you and your family are planning to attend, I would like to reserve a spot, or even two, on your dance card, if that pleases you, my Lady."

"That would be delightful. I do enjoy dancing," Lillian nodded.

"Wonderful. I look forward to it."

Lillian smiled at the lovely gift Lord Bertram had given her and shifted her gaze to him. His light brown hair was swept back away from his face, and the stubble on his cheeks and chin was barely there, and very neatly groomed. He was impeccably dressed in his daywear; his coattails and breeches were the same shade of dark grey. His crisp white shirt and cravat perfectly contrasted with the emerald-green gem in his cravat pin and complimented his skin tone.

She was not certain why Timothy did not approve of him, as he seemed to be a decent man with wealth almost as vast as her own family's. He spoke to her in a kind voice, and he was a rather attractive man.

But much to Lillian's dismay, she realized that she felt nothing in his presence. He was not the Duke.

Nor would he ever be.

CHAPTER ELEVEN

"Colborne," Samuel said suddenly, breaking the silence.

Up until the moment that he spoke, their boots on the walkway were the only sound to be heard. It was another cold winter's day, but Samuel and Timothy were dressed warmly, and the winter air did not deter them from their stroll along Regent's Park.

Samuel had several things he wished to discuss with Lord Timothy, but he did not wish to do so at Welsford House.

"Yarmouth?" Lord Timothy answered.

"I do hope that I did not bring strife to your family during dinner."

Timothy waved a dismissive hand.

"Do not be absurd. My mother can be rather theatrical at times. But it is in no way a bad reflection on you."

"Are you certain?" Samuel asked, with concern in

both his voice and on his face. "The last thing I wish to do is cause tension"

"I am quite certain."

"And your sister?"

Lord Timothy's brow furrowed, and he looked at Samuel in confusion.

"What of my sister?"

"Is she well?"

"As far as I know."

Samuel straightened his shoulders, and he was careful not to show too much concern. He did not want Timothy to grow suspicious of his interest in Lillian.

"She appeared distressed when your mother ordered her to leave the dining room."

"My sister has a curious mind and tends to ask many questions without thinking. My mother does not care much for that, and she swiftly puts an end to it."

Samuel nodded quietly, and his thoughts trailed back to the night he'd had dinner at Welsford House, especially the moment when he'd sat in his carriage and noticed Lady Lillian in her window. She was truly a beautiful young lady, and what made her even more exceptional was her curiosity. Samuel knew that he had never met someone quite like Lady Lillian before, and he wanted to get to know her better. Of course, that would never happen, since Lady Welsford had made it clear that she did not want Lady Lillian anywhere near him. He considered it to be rather unreasonable of her, as she had judged Samuel purely by the rumors she had heard of him around Town. They were not true but, despite

Lord Timothy's attempt to prove his innocence, Lady Welsford had not appeared convinced in the least.

"As long as she is well," Samuel said, averting his gaze away from Lord Timothy.

Lord Timothy grinned with amusement.

"You are concerned about my sister's well-being. Do not tell me that you are fond of her, Yarmouth?"

"She is a pleasant young woman, but I would not say that I am fond of her. I did not come to London to find a wife."

"Of course. And how goes the search for the scandalous writer?" Lord Timothy asked with a simple nudge of his elbow.

"Not well at all. I have not found anything which is of help to me. I may need to give up my search and return to Cornwall early, still bearing a wrongfully tainted reputation."

Lord Timothy stared at his friend and shook his head in disapproval.

"You cannot give up so soon."

"But I am not certain what to do. My visit to the printers was fruitless, and I am not sure what I can do next."

"Perhaps you ought to engage an investigator."

"I do hope that you are not serious," Samuel scoffed. "I would rather live with a ruined reputation than give out coin to someone who knows even less than I do."

"Perhaps they are more resourceful than you are," Lord Timothy pointed out.

"Do you know of such a person?"

"I can think of someone who knows an awful lot about finding information."

Samuel stared at Lord Timothy and shook his head.

"Please do not say that you are thinking of your mother."

Lord Timothy burst out laughing and looked out in front of him.

"You amuse me, Yarmouth. And while my mother knows of many sources who would be able to assist in your pursuit, I doubt very much that she will agree to assist you in clearing your name."

"Indeed. Who were you referring to, then?"

Before Lord Timothy was able to answer, Samuel noticed a familiar figure hastily walking toward them.

"Brother," Lady Lillian called out, waving her hand in the air.

"Colborne? What is your sister doing here?"

Lord Timothy's brow furrowed, and his jaw tightened.

"I do not know. She seems to have eluded her maid."

Samuel watched as Lady Lillian hastily approached them. Some distance behind Lady Lillian, a maid rushed after her, and Samuel smiled. The young Lady Lillian was certainly a breath of fresh air in the stuffiness of London.

"Brother, there you are," Lady Lillian said as she reached Lord Timothy and Samuel.

"Sister, you must not exert yourself so. Take a few breaths."

She nodded and looked briefly at Samuel while she caught her breath.

"Your Grace."

Lady Lillian looked beautiful in a lovely warm cape and dark brown leather gloves. Her cheeks were flushed from her brisk walk, and she breathed deeply to regain herself.

"Lady Lillian," Samuel flashed her a charming smile, which caused her cheeks to color even more. "How lovely to see you here."

"Lovely to see you as well, Your Grace," Lady Lillian smiled brightly and turned to her brother. "Pardon my intrusion. I did not mean to interrupt your conversation."

"No need to apologize."

"Sister, why are you in such a rush? Poor Meg cannot even keep up with you," Lord Timothy said, motioning to Lady Lillian's maid, who moved towards them now at a much slower pace.

"I had to speak with you, and you, Your Grace."

"What do you wish to speak of, sister?" Lord Timothy inquired and shifted his weight.

Samuel stared at her, intrigued, unable to tear his eyes away from her.

"At breakfast, I listened to Mother speak of Lady Montague's ball and how the ball was important to secure a match. Frivolous talk, really. But I am getting off track. I had a thought while I pretended to pay attention."

Samuel smiled at Lady Lillian - he found her enchanting. Every word she spoke was music to his ears, and it was true. He had grown fond of her in a very short time.

"And what was your thought, sister?"

Lady Lillian drew in a deep breath and turned to Samuel.

"Does Your Grace still wish to find the person who wrote those falsehoods?"

Samuel and Lord Timothy exchanged surprised glances, and Samuel turned back to her.

"Indeed. It is why I traveled from Cornwall to London."

Lady Lillian smiled and clasped her hands together.

"Perhaps I can be of some assistance."

"Do not be absurd, sister. You-"

"Wait, Colborne," Samuel interjected, silencing Lord Timothy within an instant. "I wish to hear what Lady Lillian has to say."

Samuel turned to Lady Lillian and studied her for a few moments.

"Lady Lillian," Meg finally reached Lady Lillian.

"It is alright, Meg," Lord Timothy said to the maid, and she nodded, stepping to the side.

Samuel suppressed a grin and gazed at Lady Lillian with a crooked brow filled with intrigue.

"Tell me, Lady Lillian, what assistance can you offer?"

"The rumors around town have caused you a ruined reputation, but you would like to restore that reputation. Correct?"

"Indeed."

Lady Lillian wrung her hands together and tensed her shoulders.

"I have a suggestion. As a result of that damage to your reputation, you are deemed undesirable by the *ton*.

Why not change that to make Your Grace desirable again?"

"Intriguing. And how would you think we could achieve that?"

"I offer to spend time with Your Grace, which will intrigue the young ladies of the *ton*. Any respectable young woman would not be seen in the company of a man with such a sordid reputation, but our family has an impeccable reputation, which would count in Your Grace's favor."

"That is how you wish to restore His Grace's reputation, sister?"

"Indeed. What does Your Grace think of my suggestion?" Lady Lillian gazed at Samuel with expectant eyes.

"And you wish to willingly spend time with me, Lady Lillian?"

"Indeed," she answered rather hastily, but in a voice filled with confidence.

"But would that not ruin your own reputation? I would not want that," Samuel stated.

Before Lady Lillian was able to answer, Lord Timothy stepped forward and shook his head in disapproval.

"I most certainly do not approve of this. And I am certain that Mother would not either. She would never allow you anywhere near His Grace, with all due respect, of course."

"Understandable," Samuel noted.

"And she would most certainly not allow her only daughter to be in the presence of a man with such a sordid reputation. The reputation of our family is the most important thing in the world to her, and she will not allow anything or anyone to jeopardize it."

"But Timothy..."

"No, sister. I will not allow this."

Lady Lillian pursed her lips, and her shoulders slumped a little.

"I only wish to help."

"And it is very kind of you, sister, but I cannot allow you to assist in the way that you have suggested. I am sorry," Lord Timothy stated.

"I understand," Lady Lillian nodded and lowered her gaze.

"I am grateful for your eagerness to help, Lady Lillian. I appreciate it more than you would ever know," Samuel said.

Lady Lillian nodded quietly and looked at Samuel.

"Will we see Your Grace at Lady Montague's ball tomorrow evening?"

Samuel shifted his weight in discomfort, and his shoulders tensed.

The mere thought of a ball or a large social gathering caused Samuel to shudder. Despite being raised by a mother who enjoyed both hosting and attending balls, Samuel had never truly enjoyed such gatherings. Parading around, dancing with young ladies, and pretending to have a good time - it was simply not something Samuel enjoyed doing.

"Lady Montague's balls are lovely, and perhaps we can enjoy a dance together as well," Lady Lillian said with a slight smile.

"Perhaps."

"I must be going. Mother will wonder where I am. Have a lovely day, Your Grace." Lady Lillian drew in a deep breath and turned away, with apparent reluctance, from Samuel and Lord Timothy.

Samuel watched her walk away from him, following the path in the direction she had come from, earlier.

Lord Timothy would not allow Lady Lillian to help him in restoring his reputation, but Samuel was very impressed with her eagerness to assist him. No one had ever selflessly offered to assist him with anything before, and he was grateful for her offer.

Even if Lord Timothy had agreed to allow Lady Lillian to assist him, Samuel would not have accepted her offer. She was a caring and delightful girl, and he did not wish her reputation to be tainted because she wanted to help him.

He would not be able to live with himself if such a thing happened.

"Are you well, Yarmouth?" Lord Timothy suddenly asked Samuel.

Samuel snapped out of his musing state and turned to his friend.

"I beg your pardon, Colborne. I did not hear you."

"You have been silent for longer than usual."

Samuel cleared his throat and nodded.

"I am well. I was merely lost in thought."

"That is understandable. My sister can get rather carried away when a thought enters her head. I apologize that I had to put a stop to her preposterous idea. It would be very risky, and I will not allow my sister to put herself in such a position."

"I understand. There is no need to apologize," Samuel stated.

Lord Timothy nodded and stared solemnly into the distance.

"Will you be joining us at Lady Montague's ball? Perhaps your presence will create redemption of some sort."

"I doubt that, Colborne."

Samuel's jaw tightened, and, despite not being the type of person who enjoyed balls, he considered attending. Perhaps Lady Lillian would have a space open on her dance card for him. Samuel was an excellent dancer, all thanks to his late mother, but he had not danced in a long while. But if he attended Lady Montague's ball, he would certainly make an exception for Lady Lillian.

CHAPTER TWELVE

Lillian was mesmerized by the exquisite gowns the ladies wore at Lady Montague's ball. Hues of green, blue, and violet swirled around the dance floor. The ballroom was decorated with an abundance of white flowers, resembling the snow outside, and luxurious fabric of shimmering gold was draped over the tables. Candles flickered around the ballroom, and it all created the perfect atmosphere.

Gentlemen were dressed in crisp white linen shirts, waistcoats in different shades, with elegantly tied cravats, all completed by exquisitely fitted long-tailed coats. She had always loved the long-tailed coats the gentlemen wore, especially in navy blue, which was a very popular choice.

Lillian herself was dressed in a lovely gown in a striking pale sapphire blue shade, paired with long silk gloves in white. Her golden locks were swept away from her face and pinned in a knot on the crown of her head, with a few curls cascading down her neck. The slippers she wore were made of the finest fabrics, as put together by Madame Periaux at the modiste's.

"Lady Montague has truly outdone herself. Would you not agree, Lillian?" Lady Welsford beamed beside her, dressed in a muted slate blue gown with embroidery on the bodice.

Lady Montague was known for her impeccable taste and style, and the balls she hosted were not only a roaring success but also the talk of the town. Her wealth and status in London, and perhaps the entirety of England, was rivaled only by that of royalty.

"I agree, Mother. It is truly magnificent."

"Where has your brother run off to?"

"I am not certain, Mother. Would you wish me to look for him?" Lillian asked.

She would much rather search for her brother than be forced to dance with gentlemen she did not wish to be anywhere near or to be paraded around with her mother.

"That is not necessary. I am certain that he will turn up eventually. I am feeling rather parched. Would you care for some lemonade?"

"No, thank you, Mother."

"Very well. Wait for me here."

Lillian nodded and clasped her hands together. She knew that her mother did not wish her to wander off without a chaperone - which was exactly what she wished she could do. Although she adored attending balls, she felt rather discouraged that evening. She was disappointed that, when she had offered to assist the Duke in his pursuit of restoring his reputation, her brother had been against her suggestion as well. She only wished to help, but clearly, it was not enough.

"Good evening, Lady Lillian."

A familiar voice said her name, and as much as she had hoped, for a moment, that it was the Duke, it turned out to be Lord Bertram. He was dressed very formally, with a dark gray long-tailed coat and a matching waistcoat. His eyes were bright, filled with an intensity that she had not experienced before.

"Good evening, Lady Lillian. How lovely it is to see you."

"And you, my Lord," Lillian nodded with a smile, bowing her head slightly.

"I could not help but notice that you are wearing the brooch which I gifted you. I am flattered," Lord Bertram uttered with a smile.

Lillian instinctively moved her hand to the brooch, and as her fingers touched it, she nodded. Her mother had not wished her to wear it at first as, generally, gentlemen did not give gifts to ladies, beyond flowers, unless they were betrothed – but then, after some thought, Lady Welsford had decided that, perhaps, creating that impression might further her own aims, and had allowed Lillian to wear the pretty piece.

"Indeed. I thought it matched well with my choice of gown."

"A very good match indeed. I am delighted that you adore it."

Lillian forced a smile.

"My mother should be joining me shortly. She is at the refreshment table."

"I am aware of her location. I spoke to her a short while ago. She suggested that I ask you to dance, which I was on my way to do."

"A dance? Is this next melody not too slow for you, my Lord."

"I cannot think of a more suitable melody, Lady Lillian," Lord Bertram smiled and held out his arm to her. The previous set was just finishing, and the next dance would start in minutes. Over Lord Bertram's shoulder, Lillian noticed her mother standing beside a friend of hers, and she encouraged Lillian with a subtle motion of her hand.

Aware that her every move would be being watched, she placed her hand on Lord Bertram's arm, and he led her to the dance floor.

"I was not certain that you would attend this evening, Lady Lillian," Lord Bertram pointed out as they started into the slow rotations of the dance, which had a great deal of turning about one's partner, and not very much of changing to other partners for short turns.

"And why is that, my Lord?"

"You did not show much eagerness when I brought it up during my call upon you."

"My apologies, my Lord. I was rather preoccupied with something that morning. Timothy and I had a slight disagreement about something, and I was still mulling it over in my head," Lillian explained.

"I hope that you and your brother are well. I am yet to see him here."

Lillian shrugged her shoulder slightly.

"We are perfectly well now. Thank you for being so

concerned. My brother enjoys making an entrance, although he is not one for these social events."

"I cannot imagine why."

Lillian tilted her head to the side, and her brow furrowed.

"My Lord. May I ask a question?"

"Of course."

"You attended Oxford, correct?"

"That is correct, yes," Lord Bertram answered with a swift nod.

"Were you and my brother friends, my Lord? I do realize that I have already asked you this, but please, humor me."

Lord Bertram hesitated for a moment and then cleared his throat.

"It was a long time ago, Lady Lillian. To answer your question, we were not, but I was aware of who he was. We did not attend the same classes, but I saw him every so often at the university. Why do you ask?"

"Curiosity. I heard my mother speak of Oxford and that you also attended. I merely wondered if you and my brother knew one another well, or not."

"I am sorry to disappoint you, but no."

"There is no need to apologize."

"But we will certainly get acquainted in the future."

Lillian subtly breathed a sigh of relief when the music ended, and Lord Bertram released her hand.

"Thank you for the dance, my Lord. I enjoyed it very much."

"As did I, Lady Lillian."

"Please do excuse me. If you happen to see my

brother, please tell him that I am looking for him," Lillian said as he led her to her mother.

"I will do so, Lady Lillian."

Lillian smiled at Lord Bertram and curtsied when they arrived near her mother, who was still deep in conversation. He bowed, and turned away, obviously seeking whichever young lady he had promised the next dance to. She breathed a sigh of relief, then turned, before her mother could pull her into whatever dull conversation she was engaged in, and made her way to the other side of the ballroom with purpose.

Truth be told, she had nowhere to be, but all she knew was that she needed to get as far away from Lord Bertram as possible. Something was rather odd, and there was a strange feeling in her stomach. How on earth was Timothy so against Lord Bertram's presence in her life if the two of them were never truly acquainted? Either Lord Bertram was lying, or Timothy was. But why would her brother lie to her? What possible reason could he have to lie to her about Lord Bertram? What did Timothy know of Lord Bertram that he did not wish her to know?

She stopped near a small collection of chairs in one corner, staring out across the room while she thought. As Lillian worked her lower lip, she noticed a familiar and very distinguished figure in the ballroom, not too far away from her. It was the Duke of Yarmouth.

Immediately, all thought of Lord Bertram left her mind.

Lillian would have assumed that a man as wealthy and attractive as the Duke would have young women surrounding him, or persistent Mamas bombarding him, but given the recent rumors, this was not true. The Duke stood alone, and not a single person looked directly at him. Their scowls were, of course, not lost upon the Duke nor upon Lillian, and she felt rather bad for him. He did not deserve to be shunned the way he was, but it did not appear to bother him. He sipped his drink and stared at the ballroom. Despite his poised stance, he appeared rather lonely.

Lillian glanced around her, ensuring that her mother was not nearby, and then she made her way towards the Duke. He looked utterly dashing in his dark formal attire, set off by a white waistcoat adorned with golden embroidery. There was, however, a pensive tension to his shoulders and jaw, which accentuated the sharpness of his features.

As she approached the Duke, his gaze shifted towards her, and his expression softened, much to her delight.

"Lady Lillian, how lovely to see you," he smiled at her.

"How lovely to see Your Grace as well. I was not certain whether you would attend, but I am glad that you have."

"As am I. You look very lovely, Lady Lillian."

Lillian's cheeks colored, and she lowered her gaze.

"You are too kind."

"Is that new?" the Duke inquired, as he motioned to her brooch.

Lillian's smile faded ever so slightly, and she nodded.

"It was a gift."

"From Lord Bertram, I take it."

"How did Your Grace know that?"

"Your brother informed me. Apparently, he is very interested in you, Lady Lillian, and I do not blame him one bit."

Lillian's cheeks colored once again, and she giggled a little.

"Pardon me, Your Grace. I do not know what came over me."

"That is quite alright. And I only speak the truth. You are a lovely young woman."

"Thank you, Your Grace."

Lillian noticed her brother standing nearby, and her brow furrowed briefly at the expression on his face. It was filled with warning, and she wondered if perhaps her mother would scold her, and drag her home if she were to stand too close to the Duke.

"Lady Lillian?"

The Duke's voice spun her back to the present moment, and she raised her brows.

"Pardon me, Your Grace?"

"Your mother certainly feels that Lord Bertram is the catch of the town."

"Then *she* should marry him," Lillian muttered.

The Duke suppressed a smile and cleared his throat.

"Have you seen your brother at all?"

"I do not believe that I have. He did not join us in our carriage, but I am certain that he is here somewhere."

She wasn't going to admit to having seen Timothy, simply because she wanted a little more time with the Duke for herself.

"Perhaps. Would you care to join me on the dance floor, Lady Lillian?" the Duke asked, and offered his arm.

"I do rather enjoy this particular dance which is just beginning – that is, of course, if your dance card isn't already filled for this?"

Lillian nodded.

"I would love to."

Lillian placed her hand on the Duke's arm and then, as the orchestra changed to the music for the next set, she enjoyed a rather spirited country dance with him. The melody was fast and cheerful, and it was precisely what they both needed to lift their spirits. Lillian chuckled as the Duke made witty comments while they danced, at least when the steps brought them together enough for conversation, and as the music ended, they were both out of breath.

"Thank you for the lovely dance, Lady Lillian. I certainly needed that."

Lillian brushed a wayward lock of hair from her face and nodded politely.

"As did I, and you are most welcome."

"I am aware of what you are doing, despite you attempting to be subtle about it. But I do appreciate it."

Lillian smiled with a hint of embarrassment and shook her head.

"Your Grace, I do not know of what you speak."

The Duke's eyes sparkled with mischief, and it mesmerized her.

Their subtle yet powerful moment was rudely interrupted by Lady Welsford, who approached them with a blazing glare.

"Lillian, come with me, please."

"Mother, I-"

"Now, Lillian."

Lillian looked at the Duke with deep apology in her eyes as her mother practically dragged her away from him and into the hallway.

"Mother, stop."

"Please, I do not have the energy for your impertinence," Lady Welsford muttered as she led Lillian to a quiet room and closed the door.

"I am not the one who was impertinent, Mother."

Lady Welsford turned to Lillian and pointed angrily at her.

"You are to never go anywhere near the Duke of Yarmouth again, Lillian. Is that clear?"

Lillian's jaw dropped, and she was shocked that her mother would behave in such a manner.

"But why, Mother? The Duke did not do the things that people think he did. He is not the man the article portrays. He is-"

"I do not care, Lillian. You will do as I say. It is imperative that you find a good match to ensure the ongoing reputation of our family. Lord Bertram is that match, not the Duke," Lady Welsford hissed.

Lillian stared angrily at her mother and threw her hands in the air.

"I do not understand, Mother. You wish me to be betrothed to a Marquess, while the Duke is of higher rank. What is better than a Duke? Should I rather seek out the affections of a Prince?"

Lillian did not allow her mother to answer as she turned on her heel and stormed off, leaving the room. She very much wished to climb back into their carriage and return home, as the night was certainly over for her, from that moment on. She would seek her evening cloak from the footmen at the front door, and she was certain that her mother would find her there, and quite quickly. Whether she would be allowed to leave the ball or not, she needed this few moments' respite from her mother's controlling manner.

CHAPTER THIRTEEN

A loud sigh escaped Samuel's throat, and his brow furrowed, creating deep lines on his forehead.

His study was quiet and peaceful, precisely how he preferred it. Unfortunately, his mind was not peaceful. The turmoil inside him was alarmingly loud, and he could not shake the feeling of dread. Not only had he not been able to find the writer of the article which had shamed him for being a gambler who was in financial ruin, but he had also realized that he might be beginning to develop feelings for Lady Lillian.

At Lady Montague's ball last evening, he had found comfort in her presence. They had shared a few moments of amusement; he had made her laugh, and he had very much enjoyed their spirited dance. Lady Lillian was a lovely young lady whose smile was radiant, and her presence made Samuel feel safe. That was a rather odd thing for him to feel. Usually, he would be the one who would help someone feel safe, but as he was shunned more and more by the members of the *ton*, she was the only one, apart from her brother, who did not turn her back on him.

Last evening, he had managed to find Lord Timothy amongst the guests after Lady Welsford had dragged Lady Lillian away, but he did not say much. They did not speak of the scene that Lady Welsford had made, despite her feeble attempts to go unnoticed. The guests, by contrast, had noticed it, and they were eager to gossip about it, pointing the finger undoubtedly at Samuel as somehow responsible for everything.

Samuel grumbled to himself as he reached for a pencil, which he often sketched with. A sheet of paper lay bare on his desk, and he began to draw.

As his mind began to wander back to Lady Lillian, his brow furrowed. Thinking of Lady Lillian was not ideal, since it seemed that she was practically betrothed to Lord Bertram. But Lady Lillian had been rather hesitant last evening, whenever Lord Bertram's name was mentioned. It was as though she was not certain of the match, and Samuel found that realization filled him with relief. He was not certain why, but he did not wish Lady Lillian to marry Lord Bertram. He was not properly acquainted with Lord Bertram, although he did remember him from university. The man had not been quite as sturdy back then as he was now - the years had been kind to him, physically, and in the fact that he had inherited his father's fortune and was doing well for himself.

Samuel certainly did not have a problem with him, but he could not help but feel envious of him. As he had come to know Lady Lillian, he had realized that, despite his vow to himself not to marry, at least not in anything like the near future, he was unable to stop himself from thinking of Lady Lillian.

As a matter of fact, he had to admit to himself that he had begun developing feelings for the lovely and lively golden-haired woman who lifted his spirits and offered her assistance to restore his reputation.

As he lowered his gaze, he was surprised by the sketch on the page in front of him. He had been so deep in thought that he had not paid any attention to what he was sketching. Yet, a perfect sketch of Lady Lillian's beautiful face graced the page in front of him. It was easy to sketch her from memory, as every line and every tiny feature of her face was etched in his mind. An unforgettable vision of beauty that called out to him, and that he was unable to ignore.

Samuel stared at the sketch, feeling rather unsettled that Lady Lillian's face was the first thing he had sketched in a very long while. She must have made a much bigger impact on him than he had initially thought. After all, she had willingly spent time with him at the ball, even if it was at the risk of ruining her family and her reputation. Not only was she painfully beautiful, but she was also selfless in that regard.

Samuel reached for the silver bell on his desk and rang it, its shrill sound piercing through the silence.

Within a short while, his butler entered the study and quietly approached the desk.

"Your Grace."

"Have you ever been in love, Billings?"

"I cannot say that I have, Your Grace. Love is a fickle thing."

"Indeed," Samuel agreed and leaned back in his leather-bound chair. "Count yourself lucky that you have not. It is a type of pain which I do not recommend to anyone."

"Is Your Grace well?" Billings's brow furrowed, and Samuel shook his head.

"Oh, do not mind me. I am merely thinking aloud. Call for my carriage. I wish to visit Lord Timothy Colborne at Welsford House."

"Right away, Your Grace," Billings nodded and swiftly left the study.

Within fifteen minutes, his carriage was ready, and, as he settled into the seat, he patted his coat pocket, where the sketch of Lady Lillian was folded and tucked away, his heart pounding in his chest. Perhaps he could gift it to her, as he was certain that she would appreciate it much more than an expensive brooch.

Once the carriage came to a stop in front of Welsford House, Samuel stepped down and approached the door. He knocked, and he was met by the family's butler a few moments later.

"Good morning. I am here to see Lord Timothy."

"Certainly, Your Grace."

The butler allowed Samuel entry and escorted him to the parlor, where he was to wait for Lord Timothy to be informed of his presence. He paced around the parlor and hoped very much to see Lady Lillian, for he could not call directly on her – not without revealing his interest to all – and he wasn't sure that he wished to do that....

"Yarmouth, what a pleasant surprise."

Samuel turned on his heel and smiled as his friend entered the room.

"Colborne," he nodded. "My sincerest apologies if I am keeping you from something."

"Nonsense. I was enjoying the peace and quiet this morning. My mother and sister are visiting a friend of my mother's. The unfortunate woman is rather ill."

"I am sorry to hear that."

Samuel was disappointed that Lady Lillian was not at home, but considered it to be, perhaps, a good thing since Lady Welsford was not there either. It had seemed as though Lady Welsford was keeping a close eye on Lady Lillian so as not to risk sullying the Colborne name – and that meant that Lady Welsford was unlikely to have allowed him to see Lady Lillian anyway, had she been present.

"Come, sit. Can I offer you a drink?"

"No, thank you. I am fine."

"Very well," Lord Timothy nodded as the two gentlemen sat on the chairs beside the fireplace. "To what do I owe the pleasure of this visit?"

"I wished to speak to you after last night. I felt that the atmosphere was rather tense after your mother took your sister out of the room to speak privately. What was said I cannot know, but it would not be difficult to guess."

"It was quite a shock for my mother to see you and Lillian engaged in such a spirited dance. And the fact that Lillian was enjoying herself immensely was also what angered my mother," Lord Timothy stated.

"Does your mother not wish for your sister to enjoy herself?"

Lord Timothy shook his head.

"It was not that she enjoyed herself, Yarmouth, but rather *who* she enjoyed herself with."

"I see. Your mother truly despises me, it seems."

"Can you blame her? Your name has been sullied to such a degree that no one would speak to you nor even look in your general direction. It was as though you were a leper," Lord Timothy pointed out.

"It is not a very comforting thing to hear, Colborne, but I do understand where you are coming from," Samuel sighed. "Is your sister well after your mother confronted her?"

"She was rather quiet at breakfast, which is understandable. She did not speak much, nor did she eat anything substantial."

Samuel lowered his gaze and was filled with guilt.

"I did not mean to cause her any trouble, believe me."

"There is no need for that, Yarmouth. My sister knew what was right, and she knew how my mother felt about her being in your presence. She brought it on herself."

"How can you be so cruel, Colborne? She is your sister. Are you not meant to protect her?" Samuel asked.

Lord Timothy narrowed his eyes at Samuel, staring at him suspiciously.

"Your furtive glances are not necessary," Samuel pointed out.

"Your concern for my sister grows each time we speak, Yarmouth. Why is that?"

Samuel shifted in his seat and cleared his throat.

"Perhaps I shall accept the offer of that drink after all."

Lord Timothy chuckled and rose to his feet. He poured two glasses of brandy from the decanter and handed one to Samuel as he sat again.

Samuel had much on his mind and quite a few things to further discuss with Lord Timothy. One of those matters was Lord Bertram, but Samuel was not certain how to approach the matter. He did not want to appear too direct, at the risk of seeming too interested in the man. Despite the unsettling feelings he had whenever Lord Bertram's name was brought up, Samuel had yet to make up his own mind about him.

"In all honesty, why the brooding expression, Yarmouth? I have known you to be a pensive man, but you have brought it to an entirely new level of late," Lord Timothy uttered, and his voice pulled Samuel back to the present moment.

"I wish to know something."

"Anything," Lord Timothy nodded and sipped his drink.

"Lord Bertram."

Lord Timothy's jaw clenched, and he averted his gaze.

"Why do you insist on speaking of him? It seems as though his name is the only name I hear. My mother speaks of him constantly, especially the gift which he has given my sister. I am certain that you have noticed the emerald brooch that she has become fond of."

"I noticed it at Lady Montague's ball," Samuel answered wryly. "It is a rather lavish gift. Is your sister betrothed to Lord Bertram?"

Lord Timothy choked on his drink, and his brow furrowed even deeper than before.

"Why on earth would you ask that?"

"Out of sheer curiosity, and... because generally a man only gives such gifts to a woman he is betrothed to." Samuel stated nonchalantly.

Lord Timothy's brow furrowed.

"As far as I am aware, nothing is official. But he has called upon her more than once."

"But they are not courting, are they?"

"Why?" Lord Timothy asked and cocked his head. "Are you interested?"

Samuel hesitated for a moment and looked at Lord Timothy.

"Do not be absurd. Why on earth would I be interested in Lady Lillian?"

"The two of you do get along well. She offered to help you restore your reputation, and you shared a rather lively dance at the ball."

"That does not mean that I am interested."

"Others have been interested with less interaction."

Samuel pursed his lips and hesitated for longer than was needed, further raising Lord Timothy's suspicions of his interest in Lillian.

"You *are* interested in my sister," Lord Timothy

stifled a laugh, but, when Samuel did not laugh with him, realized that Samuel was serious.

Samuel sipped his brandy and drew in a deep breath.

"I realize that it may be unacceptable to you since we have been friends for so long, but I enjoy her company, and I know that she enjoys mine."

"Have you asked her that?" Lord Timothy asked.

Samuel shook his head.

"Contrary to what you might think of me, I do not possess the confidence to charm a young lady with flowery words and a dashing smile."

"But let us be honest, you have a rather dashing smile. What of all those ladies who swooned as they strolled past us in Oxford?"

"That was more of a fascination."

"And what you feel for Lillian is, what, love?" Lord Timothy inquired, with widened eyes.

"Nothing of the sort. As I mentioned, I enjoy her company, and I find her fascinating. She approached me at the ball without any regard for her reputation. It did not bother her in the least that guests were whispering when they saw us together."

"I see."

"But please do not speak of this. Not to anyone."

"Are you ashamed of your feelings, Yarmouth?"

"Please, do not mock me. I am merely thinking of your sister. If word of this spread through Town, it would cause irreparable damage to her reputation, and not even Lord Bertram would want to marry her."

"Which works out well for you. You could then

marry her, Yarmouth," Lord Timothy winked with amusement and sipped his drink.

Samuel shook his head in disapproval and turned his gaze elsewhere. It was an intriguing thought, but he would never consider it. Lady Welsford would never allow that to happen, and if anyone jeopardized her family's good name, she would certainly unleash her wrath.

"I would never do such a thing. I hold her in very high regard, Colborne. And all of your family, for that matter."

Lord Timothy leaned back in his chair and studied Samuel for a while.

"What will you do regarding the writer of the rumors?"

"I am not certain, but I must do something. Those rumors are affecting my life, and I must put an end to it."

Samuel was suddenly reminded of the letter he had received upon his return to his townhouse and wondered where it was – he had put it aside, but he had been so annoyed by it at the time that he could not, now, remember where he had placed it. He recalled the very distinctive penmanship of the letter, but he did not have an inkling as to who had written it.

One thing was for certain: Samuel had to find that letter.

CHAPTER FOURTEEN

"It is not fair."

Lillian's petulant whisper went unnoticed, but that was nothing out of the ordinary. She was used to not being heard, and many times, she felt invisible. She utterly despised that feeling, and she hoped that it would soon come to an end. If she were to marry Lord Bertram, she would finally have the freedom to go where she pleased and spend time with whomever she wished. She was most certainly not a child, although her mother constantly treated her as such.

Despite not wanting to marry Lord Bertram, she would finally be acknowledged and would be left alone as well, without her mother there to hound her every day. Marriage now did not seem that terrible, although Lord Bertram was not the man she would have chosen as husband, if she had been permitted to make that decision herself.

She brushed her hair back from her temple as she sat in front of her chamber's window, staring at the quiet and dark street below. She had not left her chambers the entire day, as her mother had scolded her at breakfast that morning. Not only had she been humiliated in front of her father and brother, but she was very upset that she was not to be permitted in the Duke's presence or anywhere near him. Her mother had claimed to have had enough of her insolent behavior and had sent Lillian to the confines of her room. Lillian had not objected to that part in any manner, as she did not wish to be in her mother's presence either.

A hint of a smile briefly appeared on her lips as she recalled the lovely dance that she and the Duke had shared at Lady Montague's ball. Lillian had not enjoyed herself as much as she had that night in a very long while. Balls were no longer her favorite social events, and when she was forced to attend such an event, she would usually hide in a secluded corner until her mother dragged her away to meet another eligible bachelor who would not be impressed by her once she spoke.

It was not that Lillian was not well-spoken – instead, it was that she was too well-spoken at times, and her love for books and reading appeared to intimidate many suitors. It seemed that being a well-read woman was not desirable to men.

In an utterly frustrating turn of events, the only gentleman who was intrigued by her collection of books was the Duke, and Lillian was not allowed anywhere near him, as per her mother's orders.

Lillian sighed wearily as she gazed at the dark street. Not a carriage passed by, and it felt to her that all of the people in London had disappeared, and she was the only person left. She had never felt more isolated and alone than she did in that moment, and it saddened her immensely.

Certainly, other young ladies did not feel the same way as she did. Most young ladies she noticed at balls and social events were excited by the prospect of marriage and were delighted when any suitor showed interest. Why did she not feel that way? Was there something wrong with her? Or was she destined to be alone? She did not wish to end up being left to look after her mother in her old age. She had neither the patience nor the stomach for that.

She shuddered at the thought and shook her head. The marriage mart was a terrifying place to her, and her stomach turned at the thought of marrying a man she did not love – yet that was exactly what she was considering, just to escape her current situation.

Love matches were very rare, according to her mother, although she had experienced it. Her mother enjoyed speaking, or rather boasting, of her love match. One would think that Lady Welsford would allow Lillian to find her own love match, but as Lillian approached her third year in the marriage mart, Lady Welsford's patience had run out. Lady Welsford had found her match when she was eight-and-ten years old, and Lillian had now surpassed that age. Hence her mother's urgency to have her marry.

Lillian's thoughts were interrupted by a shadowy figure that crossed the street and walked straight to Welsford House's front door. Her back straightened, and she squinted to see better. She could not, however, see the person's face. All she was able to make out was that it was a man. She watched as the man approached the footman outside, and they exchanged words. Of course, there was no way of knowing what they spoke of. The cloaked man handed something to the footman and rushed across the street, disappearing into the shadows he had come from.

Secretly hoping that it was the Duke, Lillian rose from the window seat and quietly left her chambers. Her hand slid on the smooth wooden banister as she descended the stairwell.

She reached the bottom of the stairs, and as she approached the door, the butler came into view. Her heart jumped with fear, for she was convinced that her mother had instructed him not to allow her to move freely around the house, but he did not say anything to indicate that. He smiled politely at her, his eyes soft as they usually were.

"This came for you, Lady Lillian."

Lillian's brow furrowed as the butler handed her a sealed letter, and she took it hesitantly from him.

"Who is it from?" she whispered.

"I am not certain, Miss. The footman outside informed me of its delivery."

Lillian bit her bottom lip and nodded.

"Thank you. And would it be too much to ask, for you not to mention this to my mother?"

The butler smiled reassuringly and nodded.

"You have my utmost discretion, my Lady."

Lillian flashed him a grateful smile and quietly went back up the stairs.

Once in her chambers, she closed the door and stared

at the letter. Was it from the Duke? Did he wish to express himself in a letter, as it was the only manner in which he was able to speak to her? Although even a letter was rather scandalous, from a man to an unmarried lady he was not even courting! Certainly, he realized that her mother did not want them to be anywhere near one another, and perhaps could not imagine any other way that they might communicate.

Her heart pounded in her chest as she held the letter in her hands and thought of what a romantic gesture that could be. Falling onto her bed, she broke the seal and unfolded the page with a smile. As soon as she read the words on the page, that smile faded, and her eyes widened. She sat upright on her bed and stared at the letter.

It was not a letter filled with flowery words and amorous wishes. It was threatening and terrifying, and Lillian dropped it onto the bed in front of her. She was not certain how she ought to react to this. Her heart pounded, but not in the way that it had before. She drew in a few deep breaths, attempting to work out whether she should take the words on the paper to heart, or ignore the letter. The words had a most ominous tone to them – they were, quite simply, an outright threat to ruin her reputation if she continued to assist the Duke in his attempts to unmask the author of the article.

Quivering with fear, she climbed off her bed and paced the room until she felt dizzy and rather worried. She did not intend to show this to her parents, as her mother would overreact in her usual way and might even put Lillian in a carriage and send her to live with her

Aunt Claudia in the Welsh countryside. It had been quite late in the day when the letter was delivered, and now, she realized as she looked towards the window, it was completely dark outside. She must have been pacing for hours.

Lillian stopped pacing and dropped down to sit on her bed again, staring at the letter where it lay on the coverlet. She considered it carefully. She simply could not provide her mother with another excuse to direct her life. But equally, she could not deal with this alone – and as she also could not leave the house alone, she would need to either trust someone else in the house or wait until someone she trusted came to call. But she felt that, with this, time was of the essence. After careful contemplation, she decided to show the letter to the only person she trusted.

That would have to wait until the household was mostly asleep, so she took a deep breath to steady herself, carefully folded the letter, and slipped it into the small jewelry box that sat on her dressing table.

Not long after, a maid brought her a dinner tray, and as she settled to eat alone in her room, she was grateful for her mother's harsh requirements – with that letter weighing on her mind, she could barely force herself to eat, and to have done so in the dining room with everyone else would have been impossible. Once she had eaten, she rang for the tray to be removed, and not long after that, she called for her maid to help her prepare for bed.

Then, once her maid had gone to her own bed, the minutes ticked by as Lillian waited, acutely aware of the quiet settling over the house as everyone went to bed.

Only once she was sure that almost everyone would be asleep did she move. She folded her warm wrap around her, tucked the letter into its pockets, and left her chambers. Following the dark hallway, she was careful not to walk too loudly. Her mother was a light sleeper, and she certainly did not wish to wake her.

Lillian stopped in front of her brother's door and softly knocked. Much to her relief, the door opened, and her brother stood in the doorway with a furrowed brow.

"Lillian, why are you still awake?"

"I must speak with you. It is of great importance."

"It is past midnight. Can this not wait until morning?"

Lillian shook her head, and Timothy sighed. He stepped aside and allowed Lillian to enter.

"I do apologize if I woke you, Timothy," she uttered, but as she entered, she noticed a candle burning on his writing desk and Timothy's notebook lying open beside it. "But I now realize that you *were* awake."

"I was making notes."

"Of what?" Lillian inquired as she approached the desk.

"Nothing. It is not for your eyes," Timothy answered and swiftly moved in front of the desk, preventing Lillian from seeing what he had written.

"That is not fair."

"What is not fair is that you are knocking on my chamber door when it is past midnight," he pointed out.

Lillian sighed and stepped away from him.

"I did apologize, but this cannot wait."

She retrieved the letter from her pocket and handed it to Timothy.

"It is addressed to me."

"I can see that." Timothy pursed his lips and took the letter from her. He opened it, and immediately, his eyes widened as he read the threatening words. "What is this?"

"It is rather self-explanatory, brother."

"Where did you get this, Lillian?"

"Please, try to keep your voice down," Lillian hushed him. "It was delivered to our home late this afternoon."

"By whom?"

"I am not certain. I only saw him fleetingly, from my window. I did not see his face, but I can assure you it was a man."

Timothy stared incredulously at Lillian and shook his head.

"You do not think that this is the man who wrote those lies about Yarmouth, do you?"

"I do believe it is, and somehow, he is under the impression that I am assisting the Duke in revealing his identity."

Timothy stared at Lillian with wide eyes.

"But how on Earth would he know this? No one knows that you offered your assistance to Yarmouth."

"The writer of this letter does, and he is determined to ruin my reputation if I do not stop."

Lillian sighed and sat on the edge of Timothy's bed.

"You did not see his face?"

"No, I did not."

Timothy's brow furrowed, and he appeared perplexed.

"How did you see him?"

"I was in my room, sitting at my window. It was nearly dark outside, the street was quiet, and I was planning my escape," Lillian joked.

"Now is not the time for humor."

Lillian rolled her eyes and cleared her throat.

"I noticed a man walk directly to our door. He was dressed in black, and I was not able to see his face. Perhaps he wore a cloak. I am not quite certain. It was difficult to see clearly."

"What did he do?"

"He spoke to our footman outside, and handed something to him. I decided to go downstairs, as I thought…"

Her voice trailed, and she lowered her gaze.

"You thought what?"

"I thought, or rather, I hoped, that it may have been the Duke who wrote me a letter as it would be the only way we could communicate with one another after the ball," Lillian answered sheepishly. Timothy pursed his lips to suppress a smile, and much to Lillian's relief, he did not respond. "The butler handed the letter to me, saying that it was for me, and I rushed upstairs to read it."

"Thinking that it was from the Duke?"

Lillian stared at Timothy, unimpressed by his amused smile.

"Please, brother. Let us not get sidetracked by unimportant details."

"It certainly does not seem unimportant to you. Are you fond of Yarmouth?"

Lillian did not appreciate her brother's question, especially not at a time such as this.

"We have more pressing matters."

"Avoidance is as clear an answer as any."

"Please do not read too deeply into this. I was merely curious as to who was at our door."

"And the footman did not see who it was?" Timothy inquired.

Lillian threw her hands up in the air.

"I did not inquire. I am not allowed outside, or did that detail slip your mind?"

"You are incredibly theatrical. Has anyone ever told you that?" he smirked.

"Timothy, concentrate, please. I have been threatened by the man who is set on ruining the Duke's reputation, which he seems to have succeeded in doing with just one article. Can you imagine what he could do to my reputation or our family's?" Lillian pleaded.

"I cannot allow this. We must show this letter to Father."

"No," Lillian gasped and rushed towards him. "Please, I beg you."

Timothy was taken aback by Lillian's pleas, not quite understanding why she did not wish to involve their father.

"Lillian, this is a serious matter, and it concerns me greatly. I would feel much more comfortable showing this to Father. He will know what to make of it, and take the necessary actions."

Lillian clasped her hands together.

"Which will result in my imprisonment in this home,

a chaperone at all times, as well as not being able to go anywhere without permission."

"You exaggerate," Timothy scoffed.

"You do not have any inkling of what this may do to me if Father and Mother know. Mother has already confined me to these walls and forbidden me to be anywhere near the Duke. I cannot bear any more restrictions on my life, Timothy. Please."

"Mother is only doing her best to care for you. She has your best interests at heart."

Lillian rolled her eyes and crossed her arms.

"She has *her* interests at heart, you mean."

Timothy lowered the letter and gazed at his sister. He did not enjoy seeing his little sister in distress, and he realized that the only way to ease her worries was to comply with her request.

"I wish to make myself perfectly clear, sister. I will not inform Father or Mother of this letter, but if anything were to happen, or should you receive another letter, I must tell them."

Lillian pursed her lips and clasped her hands together. She nodded and approached her brother.

"Agreed. Thank you, brother."

Timothy held up the letter and looked at his sister.

"And I will keep this safe and away from Mother's roaming eyes."

"Will you inform the Duke of this?"

Timothy shifted his weight and nodded.

"It seems that there is no other way. He must be made aware of how urgent the matter is now."

"Very well."

"I will tell him, and together, we will find a solution. I promise you."

Lillian worked her bottom lip and lowered her gaze. Despite speaking to her brother about her dilemma, she still felt uneasy. The writer of the article, who was intent on ruining the Duke's reputation, had now set his sights on her. Terror filled her body, and she worried that she would not be able to keep her fear under control.

"I must go," she said simply and turned away.

She walked to the door and, as she opened it, Timothy said her name.

"Lillian?"

She gazed at him over her shoulder, and he stepped closer.

"Please do not fret. All will be well. I will not allow any harm to come to you, and nor will Yarmouth. He is fond of you."

Lillian nodded and quietly left her brother's bedchamber. As she made her way through the hallway to her rooms, she could not entirely contain herself, and a smile appeared on her lips.

The Duke was fond of her, and that was more than enough reason to smile.

CHAPTER FIFTEEN

"Colborne, there you are."

Samuel had begun to wonder whether Lord Timothy would join him at Brooks that evening when he arrived. Despite it being later than he had said he would be there, Samuel did not mind.

"I was beginning to think that you had better things to do than join an old friend for a brandy," Samuel said with a grin.

His grin faded as he noticed the tense expression on Lord Timothy's face, and his brow furrowed.

"My sincerest apologies," Lord Timothy said and joined Samuel at their usual table.

"Are you well, Colborne? You appear rather stressed."

Lord Timothy sighed and turned to Samuel.

"There is something I must tell you, and there is no easy way to go about it."

Samuel shifted in his chair, and his brow furrowed.

"If you aimed to fill me with concern, you have certainly succeeded."

"I do apologize, Yarmouth. It was not my intention to worry you, but it is a rather urgent matter."

"Please, do tell."

"I also wish to ask for your discretion on the matter," Lord Timothy spoke slowly.

"Of course."

Samuel grew even more concerned, and sincerely hoped that everything was well with Lord Timothy and Lady Lillian.

"This letter was delivered to our home last eve. It was addressed to Lillian," Lord Timothy said as he retrieved the letter from his breast pocket and placed it on the table. He slowly slid it over to Samuel and drew in a deep breath.

Samuel unfolded the letter, and as he read the threatening words directed at Lady Lillian, his jaw tightened, and his anger boiled up inside of him.

"Who dares to threaten your sister in such a manner?"

"We do believe that it can only be the same man who wrote the rumors of you, ruining your reputation," Lord Timothy answered.

"I cannot believe that he has the audacity to drag Lady Lillian into this mess. This is my fault. I should not have..." Samuel's voice trailed off, and he was not even certain what to say.

"It is not your fault. You were not aware of what this madman was capable of. He certainly enjoys ruining people's lives, making them squirm like bugs. Please, do not blame yourself, Yarmouth."

"How can I not? I danced with her at the ball, thus exposing her to the man who wrote the article. It was not enough for him to ruin me, now he is intent on ruining everyone who comes into contact with me."

"Do not blame yourself. We will not allow this to happen."

"Your mother surely had much to say regarding this," Samuel sighed.

"Well," Lord Timothy sighed and looked at Samuel, "Lillian made me promise not to inform my parents yet."

"How so?"

"Lillian was convinced that, if my mother and father knew of this, she would be imprisoned in our home until her last breath. She allowed me to inform you, but no one else."

"She did?"

"Indeed. She did not seem to mind at all. It seems that you two are in the same situation, only hers is more dire. My mother will not tolerate anything which would bring harm to our family or its reputation."

"Your mother is a proud woman, and relentless in her intent to protect her family. That is an admirable trait," Samuel said.

"You speak much too kindly of my mother's traits."

Samuel chuckled and leaned forward, resting his elbow on the table.

"How is your sister?"

"She is well, but despite her insistence, it is clear that she is afraid and unsettled."

Samuel's jaw tensed once more, and he felt incredibly guilty that he had brought this on Lady Lillian. It was never his intention to drag her into his situation. But the only thing that he could now do was to find the man responsible, not only for the sake of his own reputation, but for the sake of Lady Lillian's as well.

Samuel studied the letter and narrowed his eyes. There was something rather familiar about the penmanship, but he did not know why, beyond one certainty: it was written by the same man who had sent him the letter at his townhouse.

The two friends finished their drinks, but then Samuel excused himself after apologizing to Lord Timothy for cutting the evening short.

The words written in the threatening letter sent to Lady Lillian whirled through his mind as he rode home in his carriage, and he grew more and more worried with every moment that passed.

"Coachman, detour to Welsford House, please."

"Very well, Your Grace."

The carriage changed direction, and as it approached Welsford House, Samuel glanced out of the window. He noticed Lady Lillian in her window, and his heart began to pound wildly.

"Stop here, please. I will only be a moment."

"Yes, Your Grace."

Samuel climbed from the carriage and approached Welsford House. He lifted his gaze to the window and stared at the beautiful Lady Lillian. She suddenly held her hand against the glass and moved away.

Samuel's brow furrowed as he watched her disappear

from sight. Moments later, much to his surprise, the front door opened, and Lady Lillian stepped out, then closed the door behind her.

"Lady Lillian" he uttered with a smile as she approached him.

"Your Grace, come with me."

Samuel followed Lady Lillian to a dark corner in the park central to the square, hiding them from sight by the foliage of the trees.

"Your Grace, I am aware that this is most improper, but it is the only way that I am able to speak with you."

"It is quite alright, Lady Lillian, I do understand."

Samuel's heart began to race as she stared into Lady Lillian's eyes, and it was quite overwhelming to stand that close to her.

"There is something which I must tell Your Grace," Lady Lillian whispered, and she sounded as flustered as Samuel felt.

"You do not need to say a word. Your brother informed me of the letter that you received, and it was rather alarming," Samuel whispered in the shadows. He was well aware that if anyone were to see them, Lady Lillian's reputation would be ruined, but at that moment in time, he did not wish to move away, even the slightest bit. Standing close to Lady Lillian warmed his body at an overwhelming rate, but he felt not a shred of regret. "I cannot imagine how unsettled you must be feeling."

Lady Lillian shrugged her shoulders.

"Being prohibited from leaving the house as ordered by my mother has its advantages."

"Are you well under the circumstances?" Samuel asked in a concerned tone.

Lady Lillian clasped her hands together and nodded hesitantly.

"I am as well as can be expected. I am concerned about you."

"Do not be. I am perfectly fine."

Lady Lillian nodded pensively and sighed. A lock of golden hair fell onto her face, and Samuel fought the urge inside him to brush it away.

"But you need not fret, Lady Lillian. I will find the man responsible. I will not allow him to threaten you, or cause you any harm."

A grateful smile graced Lady Lillian's delicate lips, and her eyes sparkled even in the darkness around them.

"Thank you, Your Grace."

The intensity of her gaze mesmerized Samuel, and the feelings which filled him were rather overwhelming. He had not felt this way about any young woman before, and it was as exhilarating as it was terrifying. Despite knowing that he should step away, he brushed the golden lock of hair off her face, his hand gently caressing her cheek.

Her lips parted, and her chin tilted upward. Her lips were so close, Lady Lillian's breath was warm on his face, and he was unable to fight the urge that filled him. He leaned in closer to her, but much to his dismay, their moment was interrupted by the clattering of hooves nearby. Samuel moved away hastily and felt rather embarrassed for nearly compromising the young lady with a kiss.

"My apologies, Lady Lillian."

"There is no need to apologize, Your Grace," Lady Lillian uttered breathlessly.

"I urge you to go back inside before someone sees us." Lady Lillian's reluctance was not lost on Samuel, and he gently brushed away the lock of hair, which had fallen onto her face again. "Please, go," he whispered.

Lady Lillian nodded and hastily left his side. He watched as she disappeared back into Welsford House, and he sighed wearily.

It was clear that she was frightened and unsettled by the threatening letter, and he did not blame her in the least.

Of course, he blamed himself. If it were not for him, Lady Lillian would not be in this situation. He would not have brought attention to her, and the person responsible would not have set his sights on her.

As he stepped out of the shadows and went towards his carriage, he instinctively gazed up at her window. But she was not there. The candle that bathed the room in a golden glow had also been blown out, and there was only darkness.

Samuel stepped up into his carriage and directed the coachman to take him to his townhouse. It had certainly been a very long evening, and he now wished for the confines and the solitude of his home.

His concern for Lady Lillian grew as the carriage rolled along the cobblestones, and he vowed that he would unmask the man who had threatened her.

Samuel recalled the threatening letter that Lord Timothy had shown him, and the more that he thought about it, the more certain he was that the penmanship was rather unique. It was the same as that on the letter which he had received upon his arrival at the townhouse, which meant that it was from the same person.

But who was it? It was obvious to Samuel that it was a member of the *ton* and someone who had seen Samuel and Lady Lillian together, whether it was at Lady Montague's ball or strolling through the park. But it made more sense that it was a guest at the ball. Finding out who it was would be rather difficult, as the guest list had been extensive. Lady Montague had never excluded any member of the *ton* at her previous balls and, in a similar manner, had made no exception with the most recent one.

Samuel's jaw tightened as he tried to think of who might wish to ruin both his reputation and Lady Lillian's, but no one came to mind. They had no known enemies, and it was impossible to prove otherwise. Perhaps he required a new approach, but what would that be? Perhaps he and Lord Timothy ought to speak again, on the morrow.

As the carriage came to a stop in front of his townhouse, Samuel heard a commotion from outside. He stepped down from the carriage, and his brow furrowed as he saw his footmen, the Housekeeper, and a few of the maids standing outside. A broken window was visible from where he stood, and he approached his Housekeeper, seeking an explanation. The maids scattered back into the townhouse, and the footmen resumed their places.

"Mrs. Hall, what on earth is the matter? Why is there a broken window?"

Mrs. Hall's eyes were wide with fright, and she ushered Samuel into the townhouse.

"My apologies, Your Grace. It all happened very fast."

"What do you mean?"

As Samuel stepped inside the drawing room, his eyes widened. Not only was the window shattered, there was glass on the floor, and some of the furniture was overturned. Books from the bookshelves were strewn on the floor, and Samuel could not believe his eyes.

He slowly paced the length of the room and inspected the damage.

"Please be careful of the glass, Your Grace."

"Thank you for your concern, Mrs. Hall," Samuel said and turned to her. "Was anything stolen?"

"Not that we can see, Your Grace. As you arrived, we had just stepped outside to see if anything had been dropped out there, but there was nothing but the broken glass. The study is even worse than this room. We are all trying to sort through the mess. Allow me to show you."

Samuel followed Mrs. Hall along the corridor and into the study. She was correct; it was more of a shambles than the drawing room. Furniture was overturned, papers strewn about, and the drawers of Samuel's desk had been emptied on the floor. It was rather strange that the intruder had made such a mess, yet had not stolen anything of value. The priceless paintings still hung on the wall, and the Faberge eggs were still in their display boxes, but everything else had been overturned. Samuel was convinced this was not a normal robbery, but that the person responsible had been searching for something specific.

"Was anyone harmed?" Samuel asked.

"No, Your Grace," Mrs. Hall said and clasped her hands together, "although two of the maids were very much startled. They were on their way to clean the drawing room when they encountered the scoundrel."

"They saw the man?"

"Indeed. Perhaps they can give Your Grace a better idea of who the man was, although they are quite startled still," Mrs. Hall pointed out.

Samuel took a few steps, and glass crunched under his boots. He looked at his feet and noticed a broken vase on the floor, one which his mother had gifted him from France. Its delicate porcelain was in shards, entirely ruined. His jaw tightened as he crouched and touched the delicate pieces.

"Careful of the broken edges," Mrs. Hall urged.

As she spoke the words, a sharp edge cut Samuel's hand, and he winced. The glass sliced into his skin, and a searing pain erupted in his hand.

"Your Grace," Mrs. Hall gasped as she rushed over to him. She reached for a kerchief and pressed it against his skin. The kerchief was immediately stained with Samuel's blood, and he clenched his fist around the fabric. "Clara," Mrs. Hall called out to a nearby maid. "A bandage, and make haste." The maid scurried away and soon returned with a bandage. "You must be more careful with all of this shattered glass."

"Thank you, Mrs. Hall. I am fine."

"Your Grace, we should–"

"How could this possibly happen, Mrs. Hall? Where were the footmen outside? Where were you? Where were the maids?"

"I was upstairs with the maids, Your Grace. We cleaned the upstairs chambers, turning the sheets and such. I am not certain where the footmen outside were. But I could inquire."

"I will do that."

"Your Grace is pale. Perhaps some tea would help."

"I said I am well. I wish to speak to the staff. Send the maids to me immediately, in the breakfast room, where we will not be standing in all of this mess. And have Billings send for someone to board up the broken window until we can have it properly fixed."

"As you wish, Your Grace," Mrs. Hall nodded and left the study.

Samuel stared at the mess around him and sighed with annoyance. It was certainly not a coincidence that this had happened to his home, and he was convinced that it had been perpetrated by the same person who was behind the article and the letters.

Now, Samuel was more determined than ever to unmask this man, and with the assistance of the maids, hopefully, he would be closer than he was before.

CHAPTER SIXTEEN

*S*till in a dreamy state since her encounter with the Duke, Lillian sipped her tea. The breakfast room was quiet, which suited Lillian perfectly, as she did not wish to share her thoughts with anyone, least of all Timothy, who sat opposite her. He focused deeply on the newspaper in front of him and occasionally drank some of his tea.

Lillian's heart pounded as she recalled the Duke's hand brushing her cheek, and how gentle his touch had been. If she had not been terrified of being seen, she would have gathered the courage to tell the Duke that her fondness for him had grown, although she was uncertain if he felt the same. But she also recalled his desperate gaze and his promise to her that he would not allow anyone to harm her.

She exhaled slowly, composing herself. She certainly did not wish to swoon at the table. Timothy would think she had fainted, and it would cause more questions. And Lillian was not in the mood to explain herself.

Timothy paged through the newspaper, his brow furrowed.

"What is the matter, brother? You appear perplexed."

He closed the newspaper, and his jaw clenched.

"It is nothing of concern. I was merely trying to see whether there was anything else written about His Grace. But there is nothing. There was only that one article, and none ever again. Perhaps the writer has moved on, and decided to leave His Grace be. And you, for that matter."

"Timothy, quiet," Lillian hushed her. "I do not want that information to fall onto the wrong ears."

"Apologies, sister. I am merely irate, as His Grace and I are no closer to unmasking this man than we were when Yarmouth arrived in Town."

"I understand. And that I am not allowed to leave the house makes it even more difficult."

Timothy grinned at Lillian and shook his head.

"It is adorable that you think you would be able to solve this."

Lillian straightened her shoulders and raised an eyebrow at him.

"You underestimate me, brother."

Timothy chuckled and drew in a deep breath.

"I find it rather interesting that there was nothing else written about His Grace," Lillian pointed out and lowered her voice to be more discreet, "or even about me."

"And why is that interesting to you? Is it not enough that you are being threatened by this madman?"

"I am justifiably terrified, but that is not the point.

The person who published the article only did so once. He did not make any more attempts to further ruin His Grace's reputation, or anyone else's for that matter. He did, however, send letters. Not only to His Grace but to me as well. And I think I know why."

Timothy cocked his head.

"I do not understand what you are attempting to say."

"It was personal, for obvious reasons."

"Meaning?"

"Someone who was wronged by His Grace might be seeking revenge," Lillian stated.

"That is preposterous. Yarmouth would not harm anyone, nor wrong them. And he had not been in London for years. Why on earth would this person only write untruths of him now?" Timothy shook his head in disagreement. "That certainly does not make any sense."

"I am not certain as to why, but there might be someone who feels wronged by His Grace and has only recently decided to seek revenge."

"While I doubt that is possible, I will inquire of Yarmouth."

"Perhaps someone in his past. The brother of a young lady he wronged, perhaps?"

Timothy stared at her.

"That is oddly specific, sister."

"It was merely a thought," Lillian answered, and a small smile appeared on her lips.

Luckily, she had not been wronged by the Duke. In fact, she could not imagine the Duke wronging anyone. He was such a polite and kind man, who was rather protective of her as well, which only added to her feelings for him.

A light knock on the door caused the siblings to shift their focus, and a maid stood in the doorway.

"Lord Timothy, a note came for you from Fletcher House," she said quietly.

"Ah, thank you," Timothy said as he rose to his feet and approached the maid.

Taking the note from her, he unfolded it, and his eyes widened in shock. Lillian immediately noticed his distress.

"Whatever is the matter, Timothy?"

"It is from Yarmouth."

"Did something happen?" she inquired.

"The drawing room window at his home was shattered, and his study was ransacked."

Lillian's jaw dropped in shock, and she stared at Timothy.

"Is the Duke well?"

"He is. Nothing of value was stolen, and no one was harmed."

Lillian breathed a sigh of relief and nodded.

"I am relieved to hear that."

Timothy's jaw tightened, and he cleared his throat.

"Pardon me, sister."

Before Lillian was able to respond, Timothy exited the room and left Lillian behind. As she pondered in silence, a dreadful thought caused her to shudder. What if the person who had damaged the Duke's home had seen them together last eve? Despite being shielded by the cover of darkness, it was still possible that someone had noticed her and the Duke disappearing into the trees of the small park. What if it was the same person who had sent the threatening letters? Her heart pounded in her chest, and she felt rather dizzy. She could not keep that from her brother, despite every shred of her being urging her to stay silent. What would Timothy think of her?

Lillian shook her head and quietly left the room in search of her brother. She found him in the drawing room, where he paced nervously.

"Brother, are you well?" she asked.

"I am worried about the Duke, Lillian. His return to London was to be peaceful, and allow him to spend Christmas with our family. Now, it has caused you to be imprisoned at home, with threats looming over your head, and now his home has been violated. I think the correct question would be, is *he* well."

"Is he?"

"I am not certain. I can imagine that this is not easy for him, having his home violated in such a manner. It is unacceptable. Perhaps I should speak with Father and convince him to allow the Duke to stay here."

"Mother will never permit that."

Timothy shook his head.

"But we must do something. He is my friend, and I do not wish him to be in danger."

Lillian nodded and was filled with guilt. She had to say something. She drew in a deep breath and looked at her brother, who paced the length of the drawing room.

"Brother?" Lillian asked. Timothy turned on his heel

and stared at Lillian with a furrowed brow. "I must tell you something."

"Can it wait? I wish to visit Yarmouth and see if he is well."

"It cannot wait," Lillian uttered as she shook her head.

Timothy shifted his weight and stared impatiently at her.

"Well? What is it that you wish to tell me?"

"It is more of a confession, really."

"Lillian," her brother warned.

Lillian clasped her hands together and stepped forward.

"What happened was my fault."

"How on earth could it be your fault, sister?" he asked incredulously. "You did not leave the house."

"But I did."

Timothy rubbed his temples and stared at her.

"What?"

"Last eve, I sat in my window and noticed Yarmouth's carriage slowly pass by the house. It stopped, and the Duke saw me. I motioned to him to wait for me, and I met with him outside."

"Please tell me that is not true."

Lillian nodded regretfully.

"I pulled the Duke aside under the shadow of the foliage in the small park in the square. I required a moment alone with him, which was most improper, but at that point, it did not appear that way to me. It was innocent, I can assure you."

"And why did you wish to speak with him so privately that it was necessary to hide away?"

Lillian lowered her gaze and realized that her feelings could no longer be hidden.

"I wished to apologize to him and to assure him that I was well. He did not need to be too concerned, as I was locked inside our home until further notice."

"Sister, I cannot believe that you jeopardized your reputation by meeting with him in such a manner. You could have been seen."

"And that is why it is my fault. I suspect that the person who is threatening us saw us together. And to retaliate, they violated the Duke's home."

"Lillian, why would you do such a thing?"

Lillian gulped and stared at her brother.

"I care for the Duke, perhaps too much."

Timothy stepped back and studied his sister.

"You care for the Duke."

"Indeed," she whispered, twisting a curl around her finger.

Timothy sighed wearily and shook his head.

"That is not a good choice to make. I do hope that you are aware of that."

"I do. I wish I had made a different choice, but I cannot change it. But I am willing to fix it."

"And how do you think to do that?"

"I am not certain. I feel guilty for allowing this to happen to the Duke. And I wish to apologize to him," Lillian uttered quietly.

"I will inform him of your apology."

"No, I wish to do it in person."

"No, sister. You cannot be seen in his company. If the man who is threatening you both sees you together again, he might attempt something even more drastic."

"I will be accompanying you. I do not see the issue."

"Lillian, please do not be difficult."

Lillian crossed her arms defiantly.

"But I must tell him that I did not mean this to happen."

"I am certain that he is well aware of that. But as I said, I do not wish you to join me."

"The Duke is not at fault here, brother. He was a perfect gentleman. There was a moment between us that I thought he might kiss me, but he did not."

"I do not wish to hear another word, sister. It is best that you stay here. I will ensure that your apology reaches Yarmouth."

"Very well," Lillian sighed.

"I am sorry, sister, but I cannot allow this."

"Nor can I."

Lillian's blood ran cold inside her veins, and she slowly turned to the door of the drawing room. Her mother stood there, with a very disapproving and angry expression on her face. Lillian exhaled as her mother crossed her arms, glaring at her daughter.

"Mother."

"Not another word from you, Lillian. Leave us be, Timothy."

"Very well," Timothy nodded and looked apologetically at Lillian before leaving the drawing room.

Lillian grew increasingly nervous as her mother approached her, and she shivered with fear.

"Mother, I-"

"I said, not another word. Do I make myself clear?" Lillian, too afraid to say anything, simply nodded. "I cannot even begin to explain how disappointed I am with you. You not only disobeyed my wishes, but you slipped out of the house to meet the Duke," her mother exclaimed.

"But nothing happened, Mother. I merely apologized to him-"

"Harsher rumors have started from less," her mother interjected. "Do you have any idea what this could do to your reputation, and the reputation of the family? It could cause irreparable damage. What would we do if Lord Bertram were to hear of this? He would not be interested in you any longer. And then what will become of you? What will become of the reputation of the family?"

"Is the reputation of our family more important than my happiness, Mother?"

"They are equally important, but at certain times in one's life, one must prioritize some things above others."

"And my happiness does not deserve to be a top priority?" Lillian asked incredulously.

"Cease the theatrics, Lillian," her mother hissed.

"Why is it so very shameful for you that I am not yet married? Would you rather me marry a man I do not love than end up as a spinster?" Lillian exclaimed.

"Do not speak to me in that manner. To your bedchambers, now."

Lillian's lower lip quivered as she was filled with anger and sadness. Her eyes welled up with tears, but she knew that further defiance would not be accepted by her mother. She had already crossed a line, and now there was no way back from it. Her mother had tolerated a great deal of defiance from Lillian for her entire life, but Lillian realized that her mother had now had enough. Her mother's face had never before colored to such a deep crimson hue, and it was only a matter of time before her mother might suffer an apoplexy, she was sure.

"Do not simply stand there. Go, Lillian."

Her mother pointed to the stairs and glared at Lillian.

Lillian turned on her heel and left the drawing room as calmly as possible. She did not wish to make a scene or to show her mother any reaction. That would only give her mother the satisfaction of having affected her, and Lillian wanted no such thing. After what her mother had said to her, she would now prefer to be alone to manage the overwhelming emotions inside her.

She made her way to her bedchamber, quietly closed the door behind her, then turned to the window, her heart aching. The glimmer of hope that had grown inside her was now extinguished, and she was certain that it would never rekindle again. Marching to the window, she angrily closed the curtains, not wishing to see the outside world, and threw herself onto her bed.

CHAPTER SEVENTEEN

A sense of relief washed over Samuel as Lord Timothy approached him, his face filled with concern.

"Yarmouth, you are as pale as the sheets on my bed," Lord Timothy said.

"You did not need to come, Colborne. I was merely informing you of what had occurred," Samuel commented gratefully.

Despite feeling as though he was making a nuisance of himself with his friend, he was relieved that Lord Timothy had come. He had felt unsettled since he arrived home, and having his friend's presence was comforting.

"Please, I would not have it any other way. You are my friend, and I wished to see if you are well," Lord Timothy said as the two men shook hands.

Samuel winced at the injury to his hand from the broken vase and turned away abruptly.

Lord Timothy's eyes filled with concern.

"You are hurt."

"It is merely a cut from a broken vase."

"Perhaps you could use a drink," Lord Timothy offered as they stepped into the parlor.

The drawing room and Samuel's study were still being tended to after the ransacking. The two men settled into the available chairs, and Samuel felt Lord Timothy's eyes on him.

"You appear tense, Colborne."

"I am concerned about you, Yarmouth. Your visit to London has not been anything that you thought it would be."

"I must admit, it is much more eventful than I had imagined, indeed, but I am determined to find out who this man is."

"With all due respect, Yarmouth, how are you to do that? Nothing that has been tried so far has yielded any results.".

"While the man was in my home, two of my maids encountered him. They gave me a description of him, and now I have a better idea of who the man is."

Lord Timothy's eyes widened, and he appeared impressed with the progress that Samuel had made despite the circumstances.

"What did the maids have to say?"

"The man was nearly as tall as I am, with brown hair combed to the side and dark eyes. He had a short and neatly trimmed beard. He wore dark breeches and a dark coat, and he smelled of leather."

"Leather?"

"Perhaps it was his boots. I am not certain what to make of that description."

"Although it is a detailed description, it does not narrow it down much."

"It is something to work with. The maids also told me that the man had a crooked eyebrow."

"And do we know anyone with a crooked brow?" Lord Timothy muttered.

Samuel shrugged his shoulders and sighed.

"I have not the faintest idea."

Samuel ran his fingers through his hair and sighed wearily. He had not slept for the entire night, as he was assisting Mrs. Hall and the maids with tidying his study. He was rather particular about where each thing in his study was placed and had wanted to make sure of everything. The person who had overturned his study had done a thorough job of creating havoc, and Samuel felt as though his entire life had been strewn about.

"You are exhausted. Perhaps I should leave you to rest."

"Please, do not. I cannot stand being here by myself. Mrs. Hall insists on tending to my hand a hundred times a day - I understand that she means well, but it is driving me quite mad. I simply wish to be kept busy so that my mind does not focus on the havoc."

Lord Timothy chuckled.

"Someone must care for you, Yarmouth."

The two men were silent for a while, and Samuel shifted in his seat.

"How is your sister?"

Lord Timothy's jaw clenched, and immediately, Samuel knew that something was amiss.

"My sister is as well as she can be. I am aware of your meeting in the shadows, as is our mother."

Samuel's shoulders tensed.

"Colborne, it is not what you think. She merely wished to have a word with me. I did not touch her, I swear."

"She informed me of what a gentleman you were, but I was already aware of that. You are a good man, Yarmouth, and would not do anything to cause harm to my sister," Lord Timothy explained. "Or her reputation."

"Thank you. Your words are kind."

Lord Timothy cleared his throat, and his gaze grew pensive.

"She sends her apologies if your meeting somehow caused the malice done to your home."

"Why on earth would she feel responsible?"

"She is convinced that the man who is threatening you saw you together and made good on his threats."

Samuel's jaw tightened, and he shook his head in disagreement.

"She is not at fault. The state of my home is not her doing. Please make her aware of that. I carry no ill feelings towards her. On the contrary..."

"I am aware. You care for my sister. She cares for you as well. Perhaps too much," Lord Timothy stated, and Samuel stared at him in surprise. "Her words, not mine."

Samuel sighed and shrugged his shoulders.

"It does not even matter. She is not allowed anywhere near me, and your mother would certainly not be pleased if I requested to court your sister. From what I have seen, she would remove me from your home in the instant."

"I will not argue with that. I am sorry."

"There is no need to apologize. It is simply not in the cards for us. In fact, I think that it is best for me to stay away from your sister altogether. I should not contact her or drive past your home any longer."

"Yarmouth, I am certain that, if your reputation is restored, my mother will feel differently."

Lord Timothy was clearly attempting to reassure him, but it did not work.

"I doubt that. I do not wish to bring any more negative attention to your family," Samuel sighed.

"You are leaving," Lord Timothy said simply.

Samuel nodded.

"I feel obligated to. I have made quite a mess with my presence, and I no longer wish to affect others. I will remain in London for two more days while preparations are made, and then I will return to Cornwall. I do not wish to sully your Christmas any further than I already have."

"I understand, Yarmouth. I will relay your words to Lillian."

"Give me one moment, please."

"Certainly," Lord Timothy nodded.

Samuel rose from the chair he was seated in and quietly left the parlor. He made his way to the study, which looked a lot better than it had. He retrieved a letter from his desk and returned to the parlor, where Lord Timothy waited for him.

"This is for your sister. Would you kindly ensure that she receives it?" Samuel asked, handing him the letter. "It is merely a letter explaining why I cannot stay in London any longer and that I wish her the best for the future."

Lord Timothy looked struck with concern as he took the letter from Samuel and nodded.

"Of course. But would it not be better to speak to her personally?"

"Your mother will not allow it, and I do not wish to cause any more disturbances."

Lord Timothy stared at the letter.

"Lillian will be heartbroken."

"As am I, but there is no other way. I cannot allow my presence to ruin your sister's chance of finding a husband, even if that man is not me."

"Yarmouth, I am at a loss for words."

Samuel pursed his lips and nodded, the guilt filling him up. He should never have journeyed to London. The rumors of him would have faded on their own, over time, and people would have forgotten about them. By coming to London, he had given the writer of the article the power in the situation, as Samuel had walked directly into his trap. That had been the writer's plan all along, Samuel now believed. He had sought Samuel out and was now intent on ruining everyone close to him.

"I should never have come. I played right into his hands. He baited me, and I fell for it."

There was an elongated silence in the parlor as the two friends sat quietly, pondering what was to come.

Truthfully, Samuel did not wish to leave London. He had developed feelings for Lady Lillian, and as much as he wished to pursue them, he could not. He had brought enough strife to her already, and he did not wish his presence to disrupt her life any longer. She was confined to her home because of him. Her reputation was on the verge of being ruined because of him.

He could not, in good conscience, remain in London and allow harm to Lady Lillian's reputation. Despite his feelings for her, it would be best if they did not keep in contact any longer. It saddened him to imagine how heartbroken she would be when she read his letter, but there was no other way forward that he could see.

"Would you care to stay for dinner, Colborne?" Samuel suddenly inquired.

"I do not wish to be a burden upon you during this time."

"Nonsense. I enjoy your company, and your presence brings me much comfort," Samuel smiled faintly.

"Very well. That would be lovely. Thank you. I do believe that you are doing me a favor, for I can only imagine that dinner will be quite tense at Welsford House."

"Wonderful. I will inform Mrs. Hall."

Samuel rang for Mrs. Hall, and she entered the parlor.

"Your Grace."

"Lord Timothy will be joining me for dinner this evening."

"I will make the necessary arrangements, Your Grace."

"Thank you, Mrs. Hall."

As the housekeeper left the parlor, Samuel stared at the cut on his hand and sighed.

"I have been trying to think of who this scoundrel could be. But not a single soul comes to mind."

"Lillian is convinced that it is someone in your past who you have wronged," Lord Timothy pointed out.

Samuel stared at Lord Timothy, and his brow furrowed.

"Who I have wronged? I have not wronged anyone. I have not even been in Town for two years. Who could I have wronged?"

"Perhaps it was further in the past."

"I certainly made snide comments when I was a boy and played an occasional prank, but nothing cruel."

Lord Timothy chuckled.

"I recall those antics quite well."

"If I recall correctly, you were also part of those antics," Samuel pointed out with a grin.

"Indeed. But as you mentioned, it was innocent, and we were never cruel," Lord Timothy pointed out.

"Which is why I am at such a loss. It is causing my temples to throb," Samuel muttered and touched his temple. "And if that is not enough, I am worried. Your sister will despise me after she reads my letter."

"That is not possible. She is much too fond of you."

"It is because she is so fond of me that she will despise me. But I am leaving to protect her. Please do make that clear to her if my words are not enough. And please comfort her if she cries."

"I will. Although she will most certainly lock herself in her room and stare out of the window."

"That saddens me very much. Your sister is a lovely young woman, and she will make a lovely wife to someone. Lord Bertram, is it not?"

"Indeed. Ever since he received his title after his father's untimely death, he parades around London as if he is the Pink of the Ton," Timothy scoffed and rolled his eyes. "He reminds me of a peacock if I must be honest."

Samuel's back straightened, and he stared at Lord Timothy. He had not considered the man in any detail before, beyond the thought that he did not deserve Lady Lillian, but now, Lord Timothy's words, coming so close upon the discussion of their youth, had jarred what seemed to be a connection lose in his mind.

"His title?"

Lord Timothy nodded.

"Indeed. At Oxford, we referred to him as Lord William Beaumont. He was the second son of-"

"The Marquess of Bertram."

"Yes, the *late* Marquess of Bertram, now succeeded by this man."

"Good heavens. But if he was the second son, he would not have inherited that title. What happened to his older brother?" Samuel inquired with a worried expression on his face, those connections in his mind sharpening into suspicion.

He thought that he already knew the answer, but required Lord Timothy's word for confirmation.

"He had an unfortunate accident."

Samuel raised an apprehensive brow.

"How convenient."

"Indeed. The now Lord Bertram was a rather strange

young man. Prone to gambling at times, and not averse to bending the truth if I remember rightly. You don't suppose that he became willing to do more than bend the truth, do you?"

"Indeed. I recall him that way too. As far as what he may have become capable of, I can't say, but I certainly found him distasteful back then."

"It turns out that he has become much sturdier – or perhaps you could call it 'imposing' - over the years. It must be the title that caused that to happen. Or perhaps it is his ego."

Samuel chuckled in amusement, but his thoughts drifted, and he could not help but see Lord Bertram in a whole new light.

"Why did you avoid speaking of him to your sister?" Samuel asked. "Lady Lillian informed me that you said that you were not well acquainted with him."

"I did so to protect her from him. He is not the right man for her, and you and I are both aware of why. And I certainly wasn't going to go into detail about such things to my sister – it really wouldn't be suitable for a lady's ears!"

Samuel's jaw clenched, and he nodded slowly.

"Indeed."

And, as more memories of his time at Oxford, and Lord William Beaumont surfaced, Samuel recalled that he and Beaumont were not friends and even had an entirely forgettable spat about a rumor. Surely Lord Beaumont, nee Bertram could be involved in ruining his reputation? No, it was too insignificant and happened too long ago to matter to anyone.

CHAPTER EIGHTEEN

A tear rolled down Lillian's cheek, and her heart ached in her chest. It had been only a short while since her brother arrived back from the Duke's home and handed her a letter addressed to her. The Duke had explained that he was to leave London and return to Cornwall in two days time, as he did not wish to cause any more damage to her reputation. He wished them not to have any contact, and he apologized for all of the damage and discord that he had caused.

But that was not good enough for Lillian.

She wished that he would reconsider all of the things he had said, but he had made himself very clear in his letter. How could he do such a terrible thing to her? After everything they had been through, the lovely moments they had shared, how he had made her laugh, and how they had danced together. How could he simply decide to leave and wish to have nothing to do with her any longer? That was not at all what she had expected when Timothy handed her the letter from the Duke.

Admittedly, she had hoped that it was a declaration of love and possibly a proposal, a swift marriage at Gretna Green, followed by a journey to Cornwall to the Duke's estate as his wife. She had hoped that they would leave London together and that she would not have to concern herself with a ruined reputation.

But it certainly had not turned out the way she had hoped.

At that moment, she felt like nothing mattered any longer, and the hope of a wonderful life was beyond her reach. She would now have to marry Lord Bertram and stare at his face for the rest of her life while carrying the memories of the Duke in her heart.

Lillian was aware that her thoughts were rather theatrical, but she could not stop herself. Her feelings had been hurt, and she felt rather hopeless. She drew in a deep breath and ran her fingers through her hair.

She turned her attention back to the letter on her lap and stared blankly at it. The words swirled as her eyes filled with tears, and one tear ran down her cheek. Her heart was shattered, and now there was nothing she could do to stop her mother from marrying her off to Lord Bertram.

A soft knock came from the door of her bedchamber, and she wiped her tears away.

"Leave me be."

"It is me, sister. Do you have a moment?"

"I wish to be left alone, please."

After a pause, Timothy spoke once more.

"Please, sister. I must speak with you. It is important."

Lillian sighed and folded the letter, as she had been staring at the Duke's words for much too long. She rose from the chaise in front of the window and approached the door. As she caught her reflection in the mirror, she paused for a moment.

She was dressed in her nightrail, and her hair tumbled down over her shoulders. In fact, she had spent the majority of the evening in her nightrail and wrap. Her face was pale, and her eyes drawn. Her maid had ensured that she was provided with dinner, but she had barely touched it. After Timothy had delivered the letter to her, she had locked her door and pretended not to hear the previous knocks from her concerned brother.

But the loneliness had crept into her heart sooner than she had expected it to, and she craved interaction, even if it was from the one who had delivered the heartbreaking letter to her.

"Lillian?"

Lillian was pulled from her thoughtful state, and she turned away from the mirror. She unlocked and opened the door.

"What is it?"

"May we talk?"

"I have nothing to say," she stated simply.

"That may be true, but I do."

"I do not wish to hear it," she shrugged her shoulders.

"The Duke asked me to give you a message. Please. I do not wish to speak in the hallway."

Realizing that Timothy had a point, she stepped aside and allowed him entry to her bedchamber. She closed the door, locking it behind her, and crossed her arms.

"I am sorry that things turned out this way. I do not enjoy seeing you in the state you are in."

"What was the Duke's message? Although I cannot think of anything he might have wished to add to his letter. It made it clear that he wants nothing to do with me any longer. And it is for my own benefit."

"Believe me when I say that Yarmouth feels terrible. He cares for you very much. And the last thing he wishes to do is hurt you."

"But he has. I cannot mean that much to him if he can hurt me in this way, and callously leave London."

"He is not leaving to be rid of you, Lillian. He is leaving for you to be rid of him."

Lillian's brow furrowed, and she shook her head.

"I do not understand."

"He feels that he must leave before your reputation is ruined because of him. He is protecting you, sister."

"He does not need to protect me."

"But he wants to. And he is terribly sorry for all of the discord and hurt that he has caused you."

Lillian pursed her lips and exhaled slowly.

"What will happen now?"

"You return to your life as it was before the Duke arrived."

Lillian's brow furrowed, and her anger grew.

"And how do you propose that I do that? I cannot merely forget my feelings for him, Timothy."

"I understand that, but-"

"No, you do not. Have you been in love?" she asked pedantically.

"I have not."

"Then you have not an inkling of how I feel."

Lillian turned on her heel, unlocked the door, and opened it.

"Please, leave."

"No, I will not. Close that door."

"If you will not leave, then I will."

Lillian was not interested in Timothy's response, and she stormed out of her bedchamber before he was able to say anything. She charged down the stairs and marched aimlessly through the house, uncertain as to where she would care to go. In fact, she did not care much where she went; she only wished to be as far away from Timothy as possible.

As she walked along the downstairs hallway, she was met with a beautiful bouquet on the hall table. She had not seen the bouquet of beautiful white flowers before, and she stopped abruptly. She lightly fingered the soft white petals. The scent was delightful, and for a moment, it lifted her spirits.

Lillian noticed a card wedged between the flowers and quickly retrieved it. She opened it and read the name at the bottom to discover that the flowers were from Lord Bertram. The note simply said how much he enjoyed her company.

Her brow furrowed as she studied the letters on the card, and somehow, the writing was strikingly familiar.

"Sister?"

Lillian gasped loudly and dropped the card on the floor at her feet. Quickly, she crouched and retrieved it from the floor, and turned around. Timothy stood on the other side of the hallway and slowly made his way over to her.

"Apologies. I did not mean to startle you." Lillian pursed her lips, not uttering a word. She was upset with her brother and did not wish to speak to him any longer. As she glanced at the card in her hand, a thought suddenly occurred to her. "I apologize if I upset you, sister. The fact of the matter is that I also do not wish you to get into harm's way, and if that means that Yarmouth must return to Cornwall in order to achieve that, so be it."

"Brother..."

"And I am aware that the Duke cares for you deeply and wishes to protect you as well. He is only doing this to keep you out of harm's way."

"Timothy," Lillian sighed.

"Please, allow me to finish. This is important."

Lillian crossed her arms and, despite the burning questions which were quickly filling her mind, she paused and waited for Timothy to resume his monologue.

"You must understand that we only wish the best for you. It is my duty as your brother to ensure that no harm comes to you. And while it may appear that Yarmouth is cold-hearted and does not care for you, that is not the case. It is quite the opposite. He cares for you too much to allow your reputation to be ruined."

"So his intent to leave London and allow Mother to marry me off to Lord Bertram is his way of showing how much he cares for me? That does not make a shred of sense."

"It is the only way he knows how to protect you."

Lillian shook her head in disapproval.

"Are you finished?"

Timothy rolled his eyes and nodded solemnly.

"I am."

"Wonderful. Do you still have the threatening letter?"

"Indeed. Why do you ask?"

"Could you bring it to me?"

"It is in my bedchambers."

Lillian nodded and rushed to the stairs.

"Please, hurry."

"I do not understand," Timothy huffed as he followed Lillian to the stairs, then along the corridor to Timothy's bedchamber.

Inside his bedchamber, Lillian waited anxiously as Timothy retrieved the letter from the drawer of his writing desk, and brought it to her.

Staring at the letter and the note card side by side, her eyes widened, and a loud gasp escaped her.

"What is the matter, sister?"

"Look," Lillian said and showed the letter and the note card from the flowers to Timothy, side by side.

Timothy examined the pages and then stared at Lillian in disbelief.

"I do not believe it."

"It was written by the same person, Timothy."

"No, it cannot be."

"Lord Bertram is the one who wrote this letter. He was the one who wrote the article and ransacked the Duke's home," Lillian stated with the utmost confidence.

There was no doubt in her mind that Lord Bertram was the culprit. She was rather surprised that the man who had shown interest in her, the man who wished to court her, who had sent flowers to the house, and who had given her expensive gifts, was the same man who was set upon ruining the Duke.

Why had he sent her a threatening note? She could not believe that it was because of his interest in her. Yet... when she considered the matter, she was sure that Lord Bertram felt threatened by the Duke and wished to ensure that he would not stand in Lord Bertram's way, would not disrupt Lord Bertram's wish to marry Lillian. It seemed that Lord Bertram had decided that he would not allow the Duke to take the opportunity away from him. But... She was not sure – after all, the first article had been published even before she had first met the Duke... So, surely, there was something else involved – but why else might Lord Bertram wish to harm Yarmouth's reputation? It was all very confusing.

"Are you certain?"

"As certain as I will ever be, brother. Lord Bertram is the man who wrote the article and who broke into the Duke's home. It is him," Lillian stated.

Timothy stared at the two papers in his hands and sighed.

"Yarmouth and I spoke of Lord Bertram earlier this evening."

"And why is that?"

"Prior to inheriting his title, Lord Bertram was known as Lord William Beaumont. He was the second son of the late Marquess of Bertram."

"Then how did he come to inherit the title from his father?"

"He did not. When his father passed away, his older brother inherited it. A year later, his brother passed away very mysteriously, or should I perhaps say..."

"Rather conveniently," Lillian interjected.

"Indeed."

"We must tell the Duke what we have uncovered," Lillian said.

"I will go."

"I will join you," she agreed.

"I cannot allow that, sister."

"Brother, please do not deny me this," Lillian pleaded.

Timothy shifted his weight from one foot to the other, and his jaw clenched.

"Very well, but you cannot leave the house as you are."

"Of course. I will go and dress appropriately."

"And if Mother finds out, I will inform her that it was my doing," Timothy stated with reassurance in his tone. Lillian smiled in relief and nodded gratefully. "Make haste, please, sister."

Lillian nodded again and left her brother's bedchamber as swiftly as she was able to, briefly contemplating what she was to wear.

Her heart pounded in her chest, and the glimmer of hope flickered in her heart once more.

CHAPTER NINETEEN

The sound of a carriage stopping outside Samuel's home immediately caught his attention, for, until then, the house had been completely silent as he stared at the painting on the wall opposite him. That sound was followed by a pounding on the door, which startled him as he did not think that anyone would come to call, given the state of both his house after the break-in and his name.

"I must speak to His Grace at once," Samuel heard a familiar voice, and his brow furrowed.

"Is that Colborne?" he mumbled to himself as he rose from his seat and proceeded out of the drawing room.

As Samuel stepped into the hallway, he was rather shocked to see that it was, indeed, Lord Timothy at his door. He was even more shocked to see Lady Lillian by her brother's side.

The butler turned to Samuel with an apologetic expression on his face.

"My apologies, Your Grace. They are rather insistent on speaking with you."

"That is quite alright. Thank you."

Lord Timothy and Lady Lillian stepped into his home and, as Billings closed the door after them, Samuel led them to the drawing room where he had been quietly sitting, pondering the implications of his decision to leave London and return to Cornwall. He simply wished to put this entire trip in the past and never think of it again.

Of course, Lady Lillian constantly consumed his thoughts. Her lovely face and golden hair, her laugh, and the ease which she allowed him to feel. She was etched into his heart, and the memory of her would haunt him for the rest of his life - a small price to pay to ensure her safety.

Samuel had certainly been brought to point non plus, as he was unwilling to go but unable to stay. But he had no other option. It simply had to be done.

The moment he saw her at his door, everything suddenly changed. What reason could there be that Lord Timothy and Lady Lillian were at his home and so very determined to speak with him? As the trio entered the drawing room, Samuel nodded at the butler, who swiftly shut the drawing room doors, allowing for privacy.

"Apologies for the late hour, Yarmouth."

"We did not mean to inconvenience Your Grace," Lady Lillian spoke softly. "But it is a matter of grave importance."

"It is alright, Lady Lillian. Although I must admit, it is lovely to see you, despite the circumstances."

Lady Lillian smiled at him, and her cheeks colored ever so slightly.

Lord Timothy cleared his throat, and Samuel stepped back, not wishing to overstep.

"What is so important that you rushed here at this time of the night?"

"We now know the identity of the man of who is intent on ruining both our reputations, Your Grace."

"You do?" Samuel gasped. "Who is it?"

"It is Lord Bertram."

Samuel could not quite believe his ears, even though he'd had the same suspicion ever since he and Lord Timothy had spoken of the man before dinner.

"Are you certain?"

"Indeed. Show him, Lillian."

Samuel gazed at Lady Lillian and tilted his head, intrigued. She approached him and retrieved two papers from her coat pocket.

"Here is the letter that he wrote to me, threatening to ruin me if I were to be seen with Your Grace." Samuel nodded, as he had seen the letter before. "And here is a note which I found in a bouquet in our hallway. It was tucked into flowers that Lord Bertram had sent to our home.,"

Samuel hesitated for a moment as he gazed into Lady Lillian's bright eyes, and his world stopped turning at that moment. She was still the most beautiful woman to Samuel, and it was rather difficult to tear his gaze away from her.

Lord Timothy cleared his throat once more, and Samuel lowered his gaze, focusing on the note in his hand. He ignored the words written by Lord Bertram and instead focused on the curves and shapes of the letters. He studied them carefully, and his brow furrowed deeply. It was, indeed, the same penmanship - which confirmed that Lord Bertram was the culprit.

"You are correct, Lady Lillian. The same person did, indeed, write these two notes. Lord Bertram."

Lord Timothy's shoulders tensed.

"Why would Lord Bertram carry such anger towards you, Yarmouth?"

Samuel's expression grew pensive, and he felt ashamed of himself.

"It is my own doing."

"What does Your Grace mean?" Lady Lillian asked with concern.

Samuel turned to Lady Lillian and sighed.

"At Oxford, Lord Bertram was Lord William Beaumont. That was long before he had received the title of Marquess of Bertram after his father's, and eldest brother's, passing. He was not very well-known, and neither Lord Timothy nor I had any close association with him. We passed one another perhaps once or twice during our time in Oxford, and I never paid him much attention, if any."

"That is true. Why would he wish to ruin your reputation? You did nothing to him."

Samuel shifted his weight sheepishly and cleared his throat nervously.

"That is not entirely true."

"What do you mean?" Lord Timothy inquired.

Samuel drew in a deep breath and glanced briefly at Lady Lillian.

"Do you recall the rumor about Lady Bertram being involved in a scandal with a footman?"

"Indeed. It insinuated that the late Lord Bertram was not Lord William's father. That rumor spread like wildfire through the university."

"I began that rumor."

"What?" Lord Timothy gasped.

"Why on Earth did you do such a thing?" Lady Lillian asked.

"I was young and immature, and very unwise - I did not imagine that it would spread so quickly, or spread at all, given the circumstance in which it was created. It was not true, in fact, or shall I say, that we know of," Samuel sighed, angered by his own actions of the past. "I was in a tavern with a number of the other students, and someone suggested that we each invent a scandalous rumor, just to see what people might believe. We were in our cups, and thought the idea funny at the time. When it came my turn, I just picked the first Lady's name which came to my drink addled mind, and used that in my story of a woman having relations with a footman, and that resulting in one of her children being rumored to have come of the liaison. Someone else in the tavern must have overheard our conversations, for soon the rumor took on a life of its own, and spread about the town, as did the things invented by a couple of the others who were with me. It was only much later that I realized that the name I had picked randomly was Lord William's mother. I then apologized to him as I had not truly meant any harm, but clearly, he did not accept that apology. The rumor died away, like all rumors eventually do, but it took more than a year to do so."

"He has been carrying that grudge all this time?" Lord Timothy asked.

"It would seem that way," Samuel nodded. "He was, after all, shunned from all social activities. People whispered behind his back, some even within earshot of him. I felt very guilty about it at the time, and tried to start a counter rumor, that the first one wasn't true – but it simply didn't spread."

"That must have been terrible for him."

Lord Timothy narrowed his eyes at Lady Lillian.

"Do not tell me that you feel sympathy for the man, sister."

"It is quite alright if she does, Colborne. I did a terrible thing."

"But you apologized for it, sincerely. That does not mean that he should do this to you," Lord Timothy stated.

"Clearly, His Grace's apology did not mean much to the man. He carried that anger inside him for years, and it had to find its way to the surface eventually. What better way for him to release it than for him to ruin the reputation of the man who ruined his, and made him an outcast."

Samuel stared at Lady Lillian, and despite the situation, he could not help himself from smiling. He was in awe of her. Lady Lillian had been the key to solving this mystery.

"But why now?" Lord Timothy inquired.

"I can answer that," Lady Lillian replied proudly. "It was Lord Bertram's plan to lure Your Grace to London, to allow a public shunning by the *ton*. Lord Bertram knew that you would not allow anyone to sully the great Fletcher name, and that you would stop at nothing to restore your reputation. As a member of the *ton*, he could go very much unnoticed. What he did not anticipate was that you and I would begin spending time together, due to your ever-looming presence in our lives."

Samuel grinned as Lady Lillian flashed him a sweet smile.

"Of course, this was not going according to plan for Lord Bertram, and he certainly did not wish me to get involved with Your Grace, which was why he sent me that threatening letter, urging me to stay as far away from you as possible. And if I did not, my reputation would be next. That would have worked in his favor as well. Who would want to marry a young woman with a ruined reputation? Lord Bertram, of course."

"What a sly man," Lord Timothy muttered. "Yet another reason why he is not right for you, sister."

Lady Lillian rolled her eyes and clasped her hands together.

"Lord Bertram was well aware of our family's wealth, influence, and reputation, hence the threatening letter. He knew that I would not allow myself to be ruined, thus ensuring that I would not spend any more time with Your Grace. All was going according to his plan until the Duke and I were spotted together, somehow, by Lord Bertram. Perhaps he walked by or hid in the shadows himself, but he saw us, which gave him the perfect opportunity to break into your house, while he knew that you were elsewhere. What I do not entirely understand is what he aimed to achieve by doing so. Was anything stolen? Do you think that he was looking for something in particular? Or perhaps he was just venting his anger upon you in acts of destruction?"

"The maid's description of the person they saw ransacking the study matches Lord Bertram perfectly – I should have realized immediately that they said the man had a crooked eyebrow. But I agree that I do not understand the reason for that action – I am not aware of anything having been stolen, but we are still cleaning up the mess he created, so perhaps..."

"We must confront him," Lady Lillian announced and walked to the drawing-room door with determination.

Samuel and Lord Timothy's eyes widened significantly, and Samuel called out, "Wait a moment."

Lady Lillian spun around and gazed at them expectantly.

"I do not feel comfortable with you joining us in this confrontation, Lady Lillian," Samuel said diplomatically.

Lady Lillian tilted her head to the side and appeared rather perplexed.

"And why not?"

"You are not supposed to be here in the first place, Lillian."

Her brother's tone was dry as he reminded her. She rolled her eyes and turned to Samuel.

"Our parents are not aware that we have left our home."

"That certainly does not help. Your mother will be furious."

"Do not fret. Timothy has already vowed that he will take all of the blame."

"Still, you cannot come along, sister," Lord Timothy added with an apologetic expression.

"No, you cannot exclude me from this. I was the one who made the connection. I was the one who recognized the writing. I..." Lady Lillian's voice trailed off as she realized that nothing she could possibly say would sway Samuel and Lord Timothy. "That is not fair."

"You must understand, Lady Lillian," Samuel murmured and took her hand. "I do not wish any harm to come to you. It is best you that you return home before your parents realize that you are not there. I certainly do not wish your mother to be knocking on my door in a fit of righteous anger. She is rather terrifying."

Lady Lillian giggled and nodded.

"She can be quite terrifying, indeed. But I wish to do this. And if there are repercussions, I would gladly face them."

A grateful smile appeared on Samuel's lips, and he stared at her quietly, still gently holding her hand. He could not seem to let go, although he was well aware that it was more than improper. Whenever he was with Lady Lillian, he did not mind throwing caution to the wind and taking a risk as his feelings for her grew stronger each day.

"I have a thought."

Lord Timothy's voice pulled him from his thoughts, and he turned to Lord Timothy, releasing Lady Lillian's hand. He did not wish to be too forward, although he was certain that Lady Lillian did not mind at all. She was a rare gem and very tolerant of things which others would frown upon instantly.

"Perhaps you could accompany us and remain in the carriage."

"What good would that do? I will not be able to see Lord Bertram's face once you confront him."

Samuel stifled an amused chuckle.

"Your sister is truly wonderful, Colborne."

Lord Timothy pursed his lips and sighed, surrendering to his sister.

"Fine, you may come, but-"

"You will not regret it," Lady Lillian interjected.

As the trio stepped out of Samuel's home towards his carriage, the familiar sight of Lady Lillian's family's second carriage came around the corner and headed straight towards them.

Lady Lillian gasped and instinctively reached for Samuel's arm. Lord Timothy stepped in front of her, shielding her, as did Samuel.

The carriage stopped near them, and much to their horror, Lord and Lady Welsford stepped down from it.

"Oh, dear," Lord Timothy muttered under his breath.

"Oh, this is where my children are. Imagine my surprise," Lady Welsford sneered.

"Good evening, Your Grace," Lord Welsford greeted Samuel nonchalantly.

"Lord Welsford, good evening to you as well."

"It is certainly not a good evening. Where do you think you two are off to at this time of the night?" Lady

Welsford inquired, her gaze as sharp as broken shards of glass.

Lady Lillian peered through the space between Lord Timothy and Samuel.

"We were on our way-"

"Home," Lord Timothy interjected. "We were on our way home. I had an important matter that I needed to discuss with Yarmouth."

"And you brought your sister with you, despite knowing that I had forbidden her from going anywhere near His Grace."

Samuel shifted his weight rather uncomfortably, but he understood why Lady Welsford had forbidden Lady Lillian from seeing him.

"Mother, I can explain," Lady Lillian began, but her mother interrupted her rather uncouthly.

"I am certain that you can, and you will. In the carriage, immediately," Lady Welsford ordered and turned her attention to Lord Timothy. "Both of you." she turned her attention back to Samuel, "and if you don't mind Your Grace, you can send our coachman and the carriage that these two arrived in back to our townhouse."

All that Samuel could do in the circumstances was nod, and watch as they were hurried away.

CHAPTER TWENTY

*S*ilence.
The drawing room was silent, although Lady Welsford's angered stares spoke as loudly as an ear-piercing scream.

Lady Welsford had, since the moment that they had stepped into the carriage, not spoken a single word to either Lillian or Timothy, and neither of the Colborne siblings dared to speak first. Their mother was seething with anger, while their father sternly stared at them, his jaw tight.

Timothy shifted in discomfort and cleared his throat after what felt like an eternity.

"Mother, I-"

"Silence. I do not wish to hear it," Lady Welsford hissed. "Not yet."

Lillian clasped her hands together and looked at Timothy. As their gazes met, she mouthed a silent apology, and he nodded in reassurance. Despite Lillian's insistence on accompanying Timothy to the Duke's home, there was the fact that he had allowed her to. He was aware of the rules, and his mother had forbidden Lillian to leave their home, especially as she was not allowed anywhere near the Duke. It was entirely his fault, and he was ready to bear the consequences of his actions.

The carriage ride back to Welsford House had been quiet and tense, and no one had spoken a single word. Thankfully for everyone in the carriage, it had been a short journey.

Now, the two Colborne children stood in front of their parents in the drawing room, awaiting their fate. They were both well and truly of an age where they should be treated as adults, but at that moment, they felt as if they were six years old again.

Lady Welsford inhaled deeply, and the disappointment was evident on her face.

"As a mother, I am deeply disappointed."

"Mother-"

"It is not your turn to speak, Timothy. I wish to speak my piece first."

Lillian raised an apprehensive eyebrow as she was well aware of what her mother would say. Her mother found much delight in dredging up the past, and Lillian was convinced that she would do the same in this instance. Whenever she decided to speak, of course. Lillian was also aware that the longer the pause, the more dire the repercussions would be. She was already confined to her home, what worse fate was there?

"I was under the impression that I had raised well-behaved children who had grown into well-behaved adults, especially you, Timothy. You were such an obedient boy. You did as you were told without question, and you always carried the Colborne name with pride, ensuring that it could be held in high respect. You attended Oxford and made the family proud."

Lillian lowered her gaze, as she unfortunately knew that she was more of a disappointment to her mother than Timothy was.

"Lillian, on the other hand, was defiant from the moment that she was born. Even her golden locks could not be tamed."

Lord Welsford stepped forward and touched his wife's shoulder.

"We recognize the differences between you, of course, as you are two entirely different people. And we would never dare to compare you with one another."

"Only you do, Mother," Lillian managed to say.

Lady Welsford glared at Lillian, and she lowered her gaze again.

"I have never been as disappointed in both of you as I am at this very moment. You disregarded everything I had said and put this family's name and reputation in jeopardy."

"Mother, I apologize. I am the one who is at fault. I allowed Lillian to accompany me to the Duke's home."

"Why on earth would you visit him at such an hour? That is not proper, Timothy, especially not with your sister accompanying you."

"I am aware of that, Mother, and I sincerely apologize. The Duke had an issue at his home. Someone broke his window and ransacked two rooms inside his house. "

Lord Welsford gasped.

"Is he well? Was anything taken?"

"No, there was only damage to his furniture, and he hurt his hand."

"He hurt his hand?" Lillian gasped. "Why did I not see that?"

"It does not matter. Or perhaps it was due to disobeying my orders," Lady Welsford retorted.

"The more important question is, why were you two there at this time of the night? It is most improper, even if it had been only you that visited the Duke, Timothy."

Timothy nodded.

"I am aware of that, Father. I simply wished to see if the Duke was well and if he required assistance with anything."

"Timothy was being a good friend, Father. There were no ill intentions. I also only wished to see if he was well. And..."

"And what, Lillian?"

"It does not matter," Lady Welsford huffed at Lord Welsford. "She disobeyed me. What if something had happened to them? What if they had been injured, attacked, or robbed?"

"Or worse, seen in the company of the Duke," Lillian said sarcastically and glared at her mother.

"How dare you speak to me in such a tone?"

Lord Welsford held up his hands and attempted to keep the peace.

"Shall we all remain calm?"

His question was, of course, directed to Lady Welsford, but Lord Welsford was very diplomatic and did not wish to further insult his beloved wife, who had the tendency to take things too far at times.

"I am calm," Lady Welsford sighed, clasping her hands together.

"Why did you wish to accompany Timothy, Lillian?" Lord Welsford inquired.

"When he had dinner here, the Duke spoke of wishing to find the man who wrote the article which has damaged his reputation. He wanted to unmask him, and I offered to assist. Timothy, however, did not agree that it was a good idea. Nor did the Duke. He declined my offer. But I still wanted to assist."

"What did you do, Lillian?"

"She did nothing, Mother. Lillian received a letter at home, threatening her with a ruined reputation if she did not keep her distance from the Duke."

Both their parents gasped.

"Lillian, how could you not inform us?"

"What if something had happened?"

"I apologize. I am at fault. I pleaded with Timothy not to inform you. I did not wish either of you to be concerned."

"You were threatened by a man who, all evidence suggests, makes good on his promises. What were you thinking?" Lady Welsford exclaimed.

"I am not certain. Perhaps I was not thinking at all. But it turned out for the best," Lillian stated.

"And why do you say that?" Lord Welsford asked with a furrowed brow.

"I recognized the writing, and I came upon a startling discovery."

"Show them, Lillian," Timothy encouraged her.

Lillian nodded, retrieved the two letters from her pockets, and handed them to her father. He read the threatening letter first and sighed.

"This is rather unsettling."

"Read the other one, and please tell me what you see."

Lord Welsford read the note from Lord Bertram, and his jaw dropped in disbelief.

"I do not believe it."

"What is it?"

"It is the same writing – the threatening letter and the card which came with Lillian's flowers were written by the same hand."

Lady Welsford gasped.

"What?"

Lillian took the chance to explain.

"Lord Bertram is the man who wrote those untruths about the Duke in the newspaper. Apparently, he has held onto a very lengthy grudge – since his days at Oxford, when the Duke made a comment in passing about his mother and indirectly started a rumor which resulted in Lord Bertram being shunned socially."

Lord and Lady Welsford exchanged shocked glances, and Lord Welsford turned to Lillian.

"And you are certain?"

"Indeed."

"The Duke confirmed all of that with us at his home this evening. That was why we were there, as Lillian insisted on showing him her discovery."

"It was something which was only to be done in

person." Lord and Lady Welsford were stunned into silence for a few moments, and Lillian shifted her weight on her chair in discomfort. "I am truly sorry for disobeying you, Mother. I did not mean to fill our home with strife. I merely wished to help the Duke restore his reputation. And he is not the man you think he is, or the man London thinks he is. He is kind and intelligent. His wit is sharp, and he is amusing and gracious. He is well-mannered and well-spoken. He can make me laugh and put me at ease. He truly is a gentleman in every sense of the word." Lillian turned to Lord Welsford. "He was the gentleman who came to my aid when I lost my footing outside the modiste's, sparing me a lifetime of humiliation."

"Yarmouth certainly did not strike me as the type of man who had the vices the article mentioned," Lord Welsford pointed out.

"He is a good man, Father, and he certainly did not deserve what happened to him," Timothy added.

"Very well. All of these antics of yours are forgiven, but until the matter is rectified in full, I still do not wish you to be close to the Duke."

"Mother, did you not hear me? The Duke is harmless," Lillian tried hard not to speak with anger.

"Be that as it may, you still have no business with him."

"In Yarmouth's defense, Mother, the matter will be resolved soon."

"Good. I would make haste if I were in his shoes."

"I am certain that he wishes this to be resolved and

free him of the looming animosity towards him from the *ton*," Timothy nodded and stepped back.

"Lillian, I am still disappointed in you for not coming to us."

"Even if I had, I would not have been allowed to help."

"Please understand, my dearest, we only wish the best for both of you. You are our daughter, and you must be protected."

"Despite not needing protection at every waking moment?" Lillian inquired.

"One day, when you have a daughter, you will understand, dearest," Lord Welsford said, placing his hand on Lillian's shoulder.

"Perhaps," Lillian whispered.

"If I may, Lillian, why do you feel so strongly about proving the Duke's innocence? You have not known Yarmouth for very long, and he's practically a stranger."

Lillian drew in an anxious breath and briefly pursed her lips.

"I am not certain, Father. From the moment that I met the Duke, despite not being aware it was he who assisted me outside the modiste, I was unable to stop thinking of him. His warm eyes, his gentle touch. My heart pounds when I am near him, and I have never felt such feelings before." Lady Welsford's eyes widened, and she stared at Lillian silently. Lillian blinked rapidly and turned to Timothy, who flashed a reassuring smile at her. Clearly, Timothy was not concerned that she had feelings for the Duke since he was a much better choice than Lord

Bertram. His supportive nod was a clear indication that he approved if they were to start courting. Lillian cleared her throat and turned back to her parents. "What I feel for the Duke cannot be described. Mother, Father, it has taken me by surprise, and it was most certainly not planned."

Lady Welsford's brow furrowed, and she shook her head.

"Lillian, this is insanity."

"Marrying Lord Bertram would be insanity, Mother. He was the person who intentionally ruined the Duke's reputation, sent me a threatening letter because I was spending time with the Duke, and caused damage to the Duke's home. How can you even consider asking me to marry a man such as that?"

"Lillian is correct, darling," Lord Welsford nodded.

Lady Welsford sighed and touched her temple.

"May I speak with Lillian for a moment, in private?"

"Of course," Lord Welsford answered, and he and Timothy quietly left the room.

Lillian wrung her hands and drew in a deep breath. She grew nervous as her mother approached her slowly, and she feared that her mother would not understand.

"Mother, I am truly sorry. I did not mean to upset you. Truly."

"Quiet, Lillian. I do not wish to hear any more from you this evening. I am exhausted, and my soul is weary at the thought of my daughter acting the way that she does. I was aware of your defiance, but I did not anticipate that you would lose your heart to someone not deserving of you."

"Mother, how can you say such a thing? The Duke is a wonderful man."

"And you are to stay as far away from him as possible," Lady Welsford ordered.

"I do not understand. Mere moments ago, you and Father-"

"I have made my decision, Lillian. Please do not defy me again. Or you will force my hand in the worst way possible."

Lillian pursed her lips to suppress her sadness and disappointment and stared at her mother.

"And you are not allowed to leave this house, either. Do I make myself clear, Lillian?" Lady Welsford ordered.

"Yes, Mother," Lillian nodded, her heart shattering into sharp shards inside her.

CHAPTER TWENTY-ONE

"Bertram."

Samuel's voice was loud and firm inside one of the rooms at White's, and he did not care much if others noticed. Several gentlemen paused and glanced at him before continuing their conversations as Samuel approached Lord Bertram.

Samuel did not frequent White's very much, but he had heard from Lord Timothy that Lord Bertram was known for spending his evenings at that gentlemen's club. Lord Timothy had been of great assistance in locating Lord Bertram for him since Lord Timothy knew London and its people much better than Samuel did. Samuel had expected that his absence from Town would have left him at a disadvantage, but thankfully, Lord Timothy was on his side.

Lord Bertram's gaze shifted from the drink in his hand to Samuel, and despite his attempts to hide his fear, his eyes widened significantly. Samuel smiled smugly and approached the table where Lord Bertram was seated.

"You are just the person I wish to speak with, Bertram," Samuel grinned and pulled up a chair.

Lord Bertram gazed nervously at him and swallowed hard.

"And why is that, Your Grace?"

Samuel leaned back in his chair and narrowed his eyes at Lord Bertram.

"I am certain that you are well aware of my reasons."

"You have me at a loss, Your Grace," Lord Bertram shrugged and rose to his feet.

"Sit down, Bertram." Samuel's voice was firm and filled with authority, which caused Lord Bertram to sit once again. "I am aware that it was you, Bertram, who wrote those things of me in the newspaper."

Lord Bertram scoffed.

"I know not what you speak of."

"Allow me to refresh your memory," Samuel uttered, retrieving the article from his breast pocket and placing it before Lord Bertram on the table. "I will refrain from reading the entire article for you, as you are well aware of what you wrote."

Lord Bertram shifted in his seat and glanced at Samuel.

"Your Grace-"

"Please, you have said enough. And I am not in the least bit interested in your excuses."

"You ruined my social standing when we were at Oxford. I merely wished to return the favor," Lord Bertram stated.

"You admit it? You wrote the article?"

"Indeed, I did. And I would gladly do it again. Your fall from grace was rather satisfying. Hearing my fabricated lies spread through the gossip of the *ton* was most pleasing to me. And knowing that I have finally managed to ruin your reputation, hence causing you to be shunned the way that I was shunned all those years ago, brings me great delight."

"The rumor I started of your-"

"Please," Lord Bertram raised his hand and shook his head. "I do not wish to hear your apology. I did not accept it back then, and I certainly do not accept it now."

"I was not planning on apologizing, Bertram."

"Now that the tables have turned, you still remain stubborn. Why is that?"

"Because I am not the man you are. I admit that I may not have been sensitive to your fragile ego, or the possible effects of my words, and may have said things which were not true, but I did so when in my cups, as part of a students' game which called for making things up! It was done without ill intent. It was merely an innocent comment where I was none the wiser to its full impact."

"My fragile ego," Lord Bertram muttered and turned away.

"Indeed. Your attack on me was deliberate, with not only the intent of ruining *my* reputation and good name, but also that of everyone I came in contact with."

Lord Bertram chuckled.

"I assume you speak of Lady Lillian."

"Indeed I do."

"I was not intent on ruining her reputation, Your Grace. I merely wished her to stop spending time in your company. I am well aware of how important her, and her family's, reputations are to them, as Lady Welsford had made that abundantly clear to me. I knew that if I sent that threatening letter to Welsford House, and Lady Welsford became aware of it, she would have ceased all interactions with you."

"But it did not work for a while, as Lady Lillian did not inform her mother straight away."

"Indeed. I realized as much. The young woman is rather defiant in many ways. I quite admire that about her. She is certainly unlike any other young woman I have ever encountered."

"I doubt very much that Lady Welsford will allow you anywhere near her daughter, or her home after they find out that it was you who sullied my good name."

"Good name, ha. You are rather amusing," Lord Bertram laughed bitterly. "Your father had a good name in Cornwall, but here in London, there was always the echo of old rumors about his tastes, in gambling and other areas. I see no reason to expect that you are any different – men learn their ways from their fathers, don't they?"

"That is why you lured me here, where my name could easily be dragged through the mud, and where your lies would reach many more people."

"I knew that you would come. Your pride has been your vice, as well as your loyalty to your father, regardless of whether he showed you any affection or attention while he was alive, or whether he deserved that loyalty at all," Lord Bertram sneered.

"You will not speak of my father in such a derogatory manner. He was a great man."

"So I have heard," Lord Bertram rolled his eyes. "Have you finished?"

"Not in the least, Bertram. I have many questions, but the most pressing of all is, why did you set your sights on Lady Lillian?"

"Why her? If I recall correctly, I set my sights on her long before your return. It was merely unfortunate that the young lady gravitated towards you. She must have a liking for wounded and stray animals."

Samuel's anger bubbled to the surface, and he grabbed Lord Bertram's cravat and pulled him closer.

"Choose your words carefully, Bertram."

"Perhaps you two gentlemen should take whatever this strife is outside," a gentleman suggested from beside them.

Samuel released Lord Bertram and rose from the table.

"My apologies," Samuel told the gentleman, then turned back to Lord Bertram. "I will be waiting outside."

Samuel did not pause for a response from Lord Bertram; he simply left White's and proceeded to wait outside. It was not long until the door opened, and Lord Bertram approached him.

"I can tolerate many things, Bertram, but you certainly crossed a line when you broke into my home," Samuel stated. "I am still unsure of how you managed to enter my home without anyone seeing you."

"It was rather easy. I created a diversion a short

distance away. It is incredible what people will do if you offer them a few coins."

"What did you do?"

"I merely paid two men to create a diversion that was loud enough for your footmen to hear. They were on the scene rather speedily, attempting to restore the peace. I broke the window and climbed inside, then threw things around, creating a mess."

"You certainly did make a mess of things, Bertram – care to inform me of just what you hoped to find in my home? Because it certainly looked like you'd been searching for something."

Lord Bertram laughed – a bitter, ragged sound.

"Indeed I did make a great mess of the place - but there is no proof that it was me. And as far as what I was looking for? Given that Lady Lillian was still persisting with placing herself in your company, I thought to find something more to sully your reputation with. I reasoned that I might find evidence, either of your father's peccadilloes, or of your own, if you had inherited his 'tastes'. That would have given me material for further articles, to ensure that the *ton* never allowed your face to be seen in polite society again."

Samuel looked at Lord Bertram with some amazement, shaking his head.

"You were never going to find anything of that nature, because there was nothing to find. My father was meticulous with his records, and while he had some questionable tastes, they did not extend to anything easily documented – he was no fool. And I most definitely did not inherit such tastes from him – quite the opposite –

the example he provided was enough to make certain that I never indulged in any of the things he had enjoyed. You damaged my house for a foolish reason, which just goes to show how little you know about me."

Bertram almost snarled at Samuel and waved his hand dismissively.

"Regardless of that, now that your name is tarnished and Lady Welsford will not allow Lady Lillian anywhere near you, I am free to court the young woman. It will bring me much joy when I marry her, knowing that you will never have her." Samuel's nostrils flared as he grabbed Lord Bertram by the collar and pushed him against a wall, but Bertram continued to speak, despite it. "There is nothing you or anyone else can do to change that."

"That is where you are mistaken, Bertram. The writing on the threatening letter that you sent me on the day that I arrived, as well as the letter that you sent to Lady Lillian, matches a note that was attached to a bouquet that you sent to Lady Lillian at her home."

Lord Bertram's face paled, and his eyes widened.

"What?"

"I will not repeat myself. There is clear proof that you are the culprit. You were intent on ruining me and scaring Lady Lillian, with the aim of ensuring a courtship and a possible marriage for you. Simply as revenge for what I did to you, unintentionally, over ten years ago. Is that not rather extreme?"

"You do not know what that 'innocent comment' did to my reputation and my family."

"I can assure you that I do. And I do not take threats

lightly. If you do not cease all contact with Lady Lillian, I assure you, a ruined reputation will be the least of your concerns," Samuel hissed.

"Now *you* resort to threats, Your Grace?" Lord Bertram sneered.

"Indeed. The Constables will be rather intrigued to hear of your threatening letters to both myself and the innocent Lady Lillian, not to mention how you damaged my home. And I am certain that Lady Lillian, Lord Timothy, and the maids at my home would have much to say regarding your involvement in the matter. Jail time will certainly be a much worse fate than that which you initially anticipated by writing that article, is that not true?"

"You are blackmailing me."

"I am. My father may have been not at all affectionate and starved me of attention, but he taught me a very valuable thing before he passed. He told me something I would never forget, and it is this: Fight fire with fire, and one challenge with another. I would never normally resort to threats, but you have left me little choice. I will not allow you to sully my name, nor that of the Colbornes."

Lord Bertram's jaw tightened, and he nodded in defeat.

"I will leave Lady Lillian be. You have my word. She is certainly not worth all of this trouble."

"Watch your tongue, Bertram," Samuel growled. "You will also print a public apology in the newspaper, admitting that you fabricated lies about me for your own personal gain."

"Are you daft? That would ruin me entirely," Lord Bertram exclaimed in disbelief.

"I do not recall saying that you would walk away from this unscathed, Bertram. And I doubt that the constables will be very forgiving of you in prison. Not to mention the prisoners themselves. A nobleman who threatened an innocent young lady is unlikely to be received well."

"Alright," Lord Bertram agreed, defeated. "I will do what you say."

Samuel grinned in satisfaction and loosened his grip on Lord Bertram's collar. Lord Bertram stumbled backward, lost his footing on the uneven cobblestones, and tumbled onto the ground into a large puddle of water. The Marquess was instantly drenched, but he did not attempt to scramble to his feet. Perhaps it was the menacing glare that Samuel gave him which made his knees weak. Or perhaps he realized that Samuel would not be bullied into leaving London without restoring his reputation first. Either way, Samuel had the upper hand, and Lord Bertram was well aware of it.

Much to Lord Bertram's surprise, Samuel held out his hand to Lord Bertram. Lord Bertram hesitated for a moment before grabbing Samuel's arm, allowing himself to be assisted off the ground.

"I am glad that we have come to an agreement, Bertram," Samuel stated with a tight jaw, and stepped away from Lord Bertram."

"Your Grace did not give me much of a choice."

"That is where you are wrong, Bertram," Samuel spoke slowly, careful not to provoke Lord Bertram, as

Samuel was exhausted and did not wish to further the spectacle that he had already created here. "We are all given a choice in how we react to a situation. It does not matter what the situation is; it is how we decide to deal with the repercussions of our decisions that matter. You have made your choice; now, you must face the consequences. As must I face mine."

"And what would that be?"

Samuel's jaw tightened, and he straightened his coat.

"I shall be expecting that public announcement in the newspaper tomorrow, or two constables will be knocking on your door, Bertram."

Bertram nodded nervously, wiping the water from his hands.

"And Bertram?"

"Your Grace?"

"Do not force my hand," Samuel uttered before turning on his heel and making his way to his carriage. "Homeward," he called to the coachman.

"As you wish, your Grace."

As the carriage began to move, Samuel stared out of the window. He smiled to himself, but his bravery and courage wavered slightly, as Lady Lillian's face entered his mind. Was there still any hope for him there?

CHAPTER TWENTY-TWO

A soft melody filled the air of the drawing room as Lillian's fingers danced across the pianoforte. She would usually play this particular melody with a cheerful demeanor and a happy smile, but that was far from what it was that day. Today, the melody was filled with sadness and sorrow, and as much as Lillian did not wish to express in words how heartbroken she was by her mother's betrayal, she could not help the fact that her feelings spilled freely onto the ivory notes.

Despite her explanation regarding the innocence of the Duke, her mother still insisted upon her staying at home and remaining there until she decided otherwise. The revelation that Lord Bertram was the man who had written those terrible things about the Duke in the newspaper and who had also been the man who had threatened her in a letter, as well as entering the Duke's home and creating a mess, appeared lost on her mother. Lillian was not certain why, but she assumed that it was due to her lack of obedience towards her mother.

The Duke was set to depart London that morning, and Lillian was devastated by that. What if she never again had the chance to gaze into the Duke's intense hazel eyes, or hear his laugh? Would she be forced to marry another gentleman, chosen by her mother?

Or would her mother finally conclude that Lillian was miserable without the Duke, and allow her to communicate with him from afar?

These questions were unanswered, and it frustrated Lillian excessively. Of course, her mother refused to speak of the Duke, and Lillian was not even allowed to mention his name in her company.

A wrong note pulled Lillian from her faraway state, and she found herself back in the drawing room, staring irately at her trembling hands.

"Correct me if I am wrong, sister, but I do not recall the melody that way."

Lillian had been deep in thought and had forgotten that her brother was reading in the corner of the drawing room. She drew in a slow breath and straightened her shoulders.

"I made a mistake."

"That is odd. You are quite proficient on the pianoforte," he pointed out. "Particularly this melody."

"I am. I do not know what has happened to me," she sighed.

That statement was not really true - she was aware of what was the matter. Her heart was broken, which led to her poor performance with the keys. The once-loved melody filled with happiness and hope for the future was now nothing more than a sad reminder of what she had lost.

"Why do you not try again?" he suggested.

Lillian turned herself around on the bench and stared at her brother.

"I wish to know something."

Timothy did not tear his gaze away from the book in his hand but still replied.

"You always wish to know something, sister. It has been that way since the moment that you were able to speak. You have the most inquisitive mind of anyone I have ever met."

"While normally I would take that as a compliment, I am not certain whether that is a good trait to have."

Timothy's interest was piqued, and he gazed at Lillian.

"Why would you say that?"

"I feel as though my inquisitive mind has placed me in the predicament I am in now, with no way to escape."

"Tell me what you wish to know, Lillian."

"Has the Duke left London yet?"

"I would think so, yes. It is a long journey back to Cornwall, and the earlier the departure, the better."

Lillian's shoulders slumped.

"I did not get the opportunity to say goodbye to him, or to thank him for..."

Her voice trailed off and she was overwhelmed with sadness. She sniffed and wiped under her eyes.

"My apologies, brother. It would appear that my eyes still have tears in them, even though I was under the impression that I had no more tears left to cry."

Timothy closed the book and set it on the table beside him then leaned forward.

"I am sorry, Lillian. Seeing you this way brings me much sadness. It was never my intention to hurt you."

"It was not you who hurt me, Timothy. And while I understand Mother's reasoning for keeping me in the house to prevent any other scandal, it is very unfair. There is a chance that I might never get to see the Duke ever again, and it hurts me immensely."

"It is clear that it does, sister."

"I wish that there was something I could do to convince Mother that he is not a bad man."

"You have done what you could, Lillian. I had hoped for a better outcome than the one we received, but it is not always in the cards."

"Nothing I wish is ever in the cards. Now Mother will marry me off to the next eligible gentleman who walks through the door, and I will be forced to live my life pining for the one man who filled me with excitement at the prospect of marriage."

"You felt that when you were with Yarmouth?" Timothy asked with a furrowed brow.

"Indeed. I had never felt anything like it before. It was powerful but gentle enough to ease my worries. He was wonderful, Timothy, and while I am well aware that he is your friend, and possibly out of my reach, that is how he made me feel and I cannot deny that. Nor will I."

"I was not fully aware of the depth of your feelings for Yarmouth. I knew that you were fond of him, but I did not think that there were thoughts of marriage."

"It was probably one-sided, so do not fret."

Timothy pursed his lips and pondered for a short while.

"I must say, sister, I would not mind if Yarmouth courted you."

"What?" Lillian exclaimed.

"I will not repeat myself, as I am certain that you heard me."

"I did indeed. I am merely shocked at hearing that."

Timothy frowned.

"Why does that shock you?"

"The Duke is your friend, and I am your sister. He is older than I am."

"Rather older than younger, not so?"

Lillian shook her head.

"That is not the point am trying to make."

"Then what is it?"

Lillian was rather perplexed, and she stared at her brother.

"Do you mean to tell me that you would not object in the least if the Duke wished to court me?"

"Not at all."

"And why is that?" she asked, her eyes wide with surprise.

"Because I know Yarmouth, and I have for a long time. There is no man on this earth I would more easily trust with you, or your heart, than Yarmouth."

Stunned to silence, Lillian stared at her brother, and a tear ran down her cheek. Of course it did not matter what her brother had to say, or whether he approved of their relationship. The Duke was on his way back to

Cornwall, and she would never be allowed to tell him of her feelings for him.

The sound of the front door opening caused the two Colborne siblings to cease their conversation, and Lillian sighed. Their parents' voices suddenly spilled in from the front door as they entered, and Lillian pursed her lips, not wishing to speak about the Duke any longer. She was not allowed to utter his name in her mother's presence, so she turned back to the pianoforte.

As Lord and Lady Welsford entered the drawing room, they happily greeted their two children.

"Good afternoon, my dears," Lady Welsford smiled.

"Good afternoon, Mother, Father."

"Oh, good. I am delighted to see that you have left your room, Lillian. I do hope that you are feeling better," Lady Welsford spoke in a relatively caring voice.

"Quite the opposite, thank you, Mother," Lillian muttered as she paged through the sheet music in front of her.

"Mother, Father, do you perhaps have a moment?" Timothy inquired as he rose to his feet.

"Of course," Lord Welsford nodded. "Is there something the matter?"

"Indeed, very much so."

"What is it, Timothy? Has something happened?" Lady Welsford asked clutching the pearl necklace around her neck.

"While I respect your wish to keep Lillian inside our home to prevent further scandal, I do not enjoy seeing my sister unhappy."

Lord and Lady Welsford exchanged glances, and their brows furrowed.

"She is not unhappy. She is merely sulking as she is facing the repercussions of her actions," Lady Welsford stated.

"That is not true, Mother. She is miserable, and I cannot idly stand by and see my sister with a broken heart."

"What do you suggest, Timothy?"

"It is clear that Lord Bertram is no longer an option for marriage, as he threatened to ruin her reputation so that no one else would wish to marry her, and that is certainly not the kind of man I wish my sister to marry."

"While I do agree with you on that aspect, Timothy, I am not certain that I understand what you are suggesting."

"Lillian is in love with Yarmouth, although she would never openly admit it to either of you. You have made it perfectly clear that she is not allowed to bring up the subject in any way, and it has been driving her to such a deep level of unhappiness that it has started to affect me. I cannot see my sister in such a state any longer."

"But the Duke has left for Cornwall. Certainly, you do not suggest that we send someone to make him turn his coach around?"

"Anything would be better than hearing my sister's sobs at all hours of the night."

Lord Welsford approached Lillian and touched her shoulder.

"Is this true, my dear daughter?"

"Timothy exaggerates," she spoke through her tears.

Lord Welsford touched her chin and tilted it upwards. The moisture of her tears was clearly visible and Lord Welsford's eyes softened.

"My dear child. How did I not notice this? You are in agony."

"I have brought this on myself, Father. I am the only one to blame. I fell in love with a man, regardless of his reputation, and not even the rumors of him stopped me from falling in love with him. Although it did not matter whether they were true or not, I knew they were lies. His eyes were much too soft, and his touch was much too tender for it to be true."

"Men can be excellent liars, Lillian," Lady Welsford pointed out.

Lillian shook her head.

"But the Duke was not. He is a kind man, a man with integrity and grace. I have said all this before, but it did not reach your ears. You shunned him based on rumors alone, and you do not know him as I know him. You do not know him as Timothy knows him."

"It is true. The Duke is a good man, and his only vice is caring too much for people who are important to him. He protected Lillian by telling her that they should not have any more contact. That was why he wished to leave London; he was trying to keep Lillian from harm."

Lord Welsford glanced at Lady Welsford and cleared his throat.

"It appears that you have acted rather rashly when it came to Yarmouth."

"I was merely protecting our daughter," Lady Welsford defended.

"And while I appreciate that, my dear, I agree with Timothy. It is not fair to Lillian to keep her here at home. And for her to be as miserable as she is."

"I was not going to allow her to marry Lord Bertram either, if you must know. I heard from Lady Montague that he does not possess the fortune and good name that we initially believed he had. Not that it matters, since Lillian was never truly interested in becoming his wife."

"Not in the least, Mother."

Loud footsteps were heard in the hallway and a footman cleared his throat.

"Pardon the interruption, but there is a caller for Lady Lillian."

Lord and Lady Welsford exchanged perplexed glances and even Lillian frowned at the news.

"I am not in any mood to entertain Lord Bertram, or anyone for that matter, Peters," Lillian sighed.

"Not even me?"

The deep, baritone voice of the Duke filled the air, and Lillian immediately rose to her feet. As their gazes met, Lillian's heart raced in her chest. The sight of the Duke was truly a welcome one indeed.

CHAPTER TWENTY-THREE

Samuel was pleased with the way that Lady Lillian's face lit up as he stepped into the drawing-room, but he still noticed the puffiness under her eyes. The young lady had been crying, and he wished to fix that immediately. He felt rather nervous as both Lord and Lady Welsford were present, as well as Lord Timothy, but it was a relief to him as well. He finally had the opportunity to say what was in his heart with everyone present.

"My sincerest apologies for the abrupt intrusion, my Lord and my Lady."

"According to my knowledge, were you not supposed to be on your way back to Cornwall?" Lord Timothy inquired as he approached Samuel and shook his hand with a content smile on his face.

"I had planned to be, but there were too many things left unsaid, and I wished to rectify that."

Samuel briefly glanced at Lady Lillian before he turned to Lord and Lady Welsford.

"Say what you wish to say, Your Grace," Lord Welsford nodded.

Samuel smiled gratefully and stepped forward, clasping his hands together.

"For the longest time, I felt isolated, as if I never truly belonged anywhere. The untimely death of my parents certainly did not do me any favors either. I was alone at my home in Cornwall, and my life was bleak. Until I arrived back in London." Samuel turned to gaze at Lady Lillian as her eyes sparkled, a hint of a smile on her lips. "Of course, I was here for an entirely different reason, but a young lady fell into my arms and I caught her, and I was, thereafter, unable to focus my attention on anything else. She occupied my thoughts, and I could not stop myself from ordering my carriage to drive past her home."

"Your Grace-"

"I have not finished, my Lord," Samuel interrupted. "I am certain that you are all aware that Lord Bertram was behind the rumors which threatened to permanently ruin my reputation, forcing me back to Cornwall. But I will not allow him to do whatever he wishes. As a matter of fact, I believe that I am the one with the upper hand, as I have now had a very long conversation with the Marquess, who, as a result, understands the error of his ways."

"Your Grace spoke with Lord Bertram?" Lady Welsford inquired.

"Indeed. And I am quite happy to say that he has made a very public gesture of apology in this morning's newspaper."

Samuel handed the newspaper to Lord Welsford and

pointed to the article. Lord and Lady Welsford quietly read the public apology written by Lord Bertram, and their eyes widened.

"He made a public apology, retracting everything which he had written previously?"

Lord Timothy gasped and approached his father, seeking to read the paper.

"Indeed," Samuel nodded.

"How on earth did you manage that?" Lord Timothy asked.

"I was rather persuasive," Samuel grinned and briefly looked at Lady Lillian.

Her smile warmed his heart, and he winked at her. Lady Lillian's cheeks colored slightly, and she lowered her gaze.

"That is wonderful, Your Grace. I still do not understand why you are still here in London."

"A few reasons. First of all, Lord Timothy invited me to spend Christmas with your family, and I felt that it would be most rude of me if I were to leave prematurely. Despite the rumors, Lord Timothy was still a very good friend to me and was confident in my innocence. As was Lady Lillian. She even offered to assist me in restoring my reputation, which I declined, not by any fault of your daughter. She is a wonderful young woman, and I would have gladly enlisted her assistance if it had not held the risk of bringing any harm to her. That was why I declined her offer. I did not wish for her to be harmed in any way."

"That is very noble of you, Your Grace."

"I had come to London looking for the man who was set on ruining me, but my journey here has set new things in my path. Things that I never expected, but I am most delighted to experience." Lady Lillian's quiet smile was enough to cause Samuel's heart to pound wildly in his chest, as his love for Lady Lillian was far too magnificent to contain. "And lastly, I could not bear to leave London, as I would be denying myself something which I had never anticipated I would feel. And that is love."

Lady Lillian's eyes widened, and her lips parted.

"Love, Your Grace?" Lord Welsford inquired.

"Indeed, my Lord. The only emotion that has the strength to make heroes of men and change the world for the better. My Lord, my Lady, I am in love with your daughter, and I cannot ignore my feelings. I wish to ask your permission to court your daughter, as the thought of leaving, of being away from her, is truly unbearable to me."

Lord Timothy smiled and stepped away from his parents. He approached Samuel and stared at him.

"I am certainly not the man of the house, but I see no problem with granting the Duke his request. What say you, Father?"

Lord Welsford cleared his throat and stepped forward.

"While I certainly appreciate that Your Grace came here and asked for my permission in person, I believe that you have forgotten something rather important."

Samuel's brow furrowed, and his hands dropped to his sides.

"And what might that be, my Lord?"

"My daughter's permission," Lord Welsford answered. "My only wish for my daughter is that she is happy, and I do believe that, a short while ago, she expressed herself very clearly regarding her feelings for Your Grace."

Samuel's brows shot up, and he turned to Lady Lillian.

"Is that so?"

"Indeed," Lillian nodded and slowly approached Samuel.

"And in what manner did you express yourself so very clearly?"

Lady Lillian smiled, and Samuel held out his hand to her. She took it, and he squeezed her hand gently.

"If you must know, I shared a piece of my heart with my family. I have never known such feelings, prior to meeting you. Even when I did not know who you were, outside the modiste's, there was something about you that spoke to me. Your kind eyes, the warmth of your touch, and the ease of your presence made our first meeting very unforgettable. And it made *you* very unforgettable."

"Your words are kind, Lady Lillian," Samuel smiled and lowered his gaze.

"They are truthful, Your Grace. I have not met a man who could compete with you. I have thought of you incessantly from the moment that we met, and the times we spent together were truly delightful. And you are a wonderful dancer, despite not thinking so."

Samuel smiled happily and took both of Lady Lillian's hands in his. He tenderly stroked her soft skin and gazed deeply into her eyes.

"Lady Lillian, I wish to court you, if you allow me to."

Lady Lillian briefly gazed at her parents and Lord

Timothy, who smiled with encouragement and reassurance. Their support meant a great deal to Lady Lillian, Samuel could see, and she nodded.

Turning her attention back to Samuel, she drew in a deep breath.

"I would very much like that, Your Grace."

Samuel squeezed her hand lightly, and his smile widened even more.

"I am delighted to hear that, Lady Lillian"

"Now you truly are part of the family, Yarmouth."

Samuel's brow furrowed, and he turned to Lord Timothy.

"I was under the impression I already was."

Lord Timothy chuckled as Lord Welsford came to stand in front of Samuel.

"Your Grace."

"Lord Welsford. I must apologize for the disruption which I have caused your family," Samuel uttered. "It was most certainly not my intention."

Lord Welsford shook his head.

"Please, do not apologize, Your Grace. Winters are dreary as it is, and you simply brought some excitement to it. I am certainly not complaining, and I am most grateful that it was an eventful time."

"Eventful is not the word I would use," Lady Welsford pointed out.

Samuel turned to Lady Welsford and nodded apologetically.

"Lady Welsford, I do feel as though I owe you an apology as well. I am well aware that you only wish for your daughter's happiness, but I can assure you that I do as well. And I apologize for any discomfort or ill feelings I have caused during my stay in London."

"That is alright, Your Grace. Perhaps I judged you rather hastily and acted rashly because of my fear for Lillian's reputation. As well as the reputation of my family," Lady Welsford spoke with care. "I do hope that Your Grace understands why I acted the way that I did, although I must apologize if I offended Your Grace in any manner."

Samuel smiled and shifted his weight from one side to the other.

"My Lady, all is well. You were protecting your family, and anyone in your position would have done the same. I do not place any blame on you at all. It showed me that you love your family so much that you are willing to do whatever is necessary to protect them. That is a wonderful trait to have, my Lady. And I am in awe of you. That is certainly where we are similar. I am also willing to do anything for the people I love."

"Thank you, Your Grace," Lady Welsford smiled gratefully. "And I am sorry for the things that I said to you, and the way that I treated you."

"Do not fret. All is well, my Lady. I am merely thankful that this terrible situation is now behind us, and we can move forward to a better time, and one assuredly more joyous."

"Indeed," Lord Timothy agreed.

"You are not upset, my friend, that I have feelings for your sister?" Samuel inquired.

Lord Timothy gazed at him, a perplexed expression on his face.

"Why on earth would I be upset?"

"You and I have been friends a long while, and we promised one another that we would not allow anything to influence our friendship. Even through the years where we were apart and only able to keep in contact with letters, our friendship remained perfectly intact, as though we had never been apart from one another."

"Yarmouth, there is no one on this earth who I trust more than you. It is true; we have been friends for a long while. We stood by one another's side at Oxford and have done so ever since. You are the best person I know, and I wish only for your happiness. I see the way that Lillian gazes upon you, and ever since you met her, there has been a sparkle in your eyes that I have never seen before. But it gladdens my heart to see you happy, and please believe me when I say this. There is no better man for my sister than you, and there is no better woman for you than my sister."

Samuel grinned happily, touched deeply by his best friend's words. He had never been praised as highly as Lord Timothy had just praised him, and he was truly grateful that he had a friend like Lord Timothy in his life.

"Your words mean the world to me, Colborne."

"And I trust that I will not be required to keep you in line."

"You will not. Your sister will gladly do that on everyone's behalf."

"Your Grace?"

The sound of Lady Lillian's voice immediately caught Samuel's attention, and he turned towards her.

"Lady Lillian."

Her smile was bright and intoxicating, and Samuel could not stop himself from gazing upon her with awe and love.

"Does this mean that you will not be returning to Cornwall?" she asked with bright eyes.

"Not for the time being, Lady Lillian. As planned, I look forward to spending Christmas with you and your family."

Lillian's face lit up with joy, and he took her hand, squeezing it lightly.

Upon his arrival in London a fortnight ago, he would have never anticipated that, even as he went about finding the writer of the derogatory article, he would also find the love of his life.

CHAPTER TWENTY-FOUR

The cold air blew lightly at Lillian as she and her parents, along with Timothy, stepped out of the Abbey after the service on Christmas morning. The Colborne family had attended the service together, which was not a common occurrence, but given the events of late, the family had grown closer. Some might think that such scandalous things would tear a family apart, but their tolerance for one another was impressive. Luckily, Lord Welsford was rather skilled at being the peacemaker in the family. Even Lillian and her mother had spent much time speaking to one another, and things were well between them.

They were dressed warmly in winter coats, and Lillian's hands were wrapped in her favorite fur muff, keeping the cold at bay. After the family greeted acquaintances, they made their way to their coach, as they did not wish to engage in any gossip. They had certainly had a more than large enough share of gossip to last them the rest of the year and well into Spring.

"Lillian, I was under the impression that the Duke would join us this morning," Lady Welsford said with a questioning glance, although there was nothing malicious about her statement.

Much to Lillian and everyone else's surprise, Lady Welsford had warmed up to the Duke over the past few days, and it was such a relief to Lillian. She could not have borne it if her mother had continued to disapprove of the man who courted her, and who she was smitten with. Of course, the Duke had done his part to impress her mother, and he continued to flatter her for the tiniest of things, which Lady Welsford found most enjoyable. Any woman would feel flattered and flustered if a man such as the Duke were to hand out so many compliments. Of course, these compliments were all sincere, which made it even more endearing to Lillian who had previously worried that her mother would never truly accept the Duke. She was pleasantly surprised by how rapidly her mother had progressed from barely tolerating the Duke for the sake of Timothy, to growing fond of him, and more so with every day that passed.

As they walked to their coach, Lillian gazed at her mother.

"His Grace informed me that he had an errand to run this morning and will be joining us shortly."

"An errand on Christmas Day? Whatever was more important than Morning Service at the Abbey?" Lady Welsford asked.

"I am certain that it was important to His Grace, Mother."

"Indeed. The Duke is aware of what is important and

what is not. The man has his priorities in order," Lord Welsford agreed.

Of course, her father had not a bad word to say about the Duke. The two men got along swimmingly and discussed various topics, from politics to business and everything in between. The Duke was particularly enthralled by Lord Welsford's stories of his travels when he was a young man. Of course, he had not travelled after he married Lady Welsford, and after the children were born. Yarmouth would spend hours listening to the tales of Lord Welsford's travels and, he had told her, had hopes of traveling one day, hopefully with Lillian by his side.

Timothy nudged Lillian and grinned.

"Speaking of Yarmouth, here he is now."

Lillian's heart instantly sped up as she noticed the Duke approaching her. Dressed in light-colored breeches, boots, and a bottle-green double-breasted long-tail coat with a crisp white cravat, the Duke was utterly dashing. And quite coincidentally, the shade of his coat matched Lillian's dress perfectly, as though they were made for one another.

His handsome face caused heat to rise inside her body, and her cheeks flushed at the mere sight of him. A playful grin appeared on his lips, and his eyes lit up when he saw her.

"Lillian, we shall wait in the coach for you," Lady Welsford whispered as she touched Lillian's shoulder, allowing Lillian and the Duke a moment alone.

"I am fairly certain that Lillian will be riding with the Duke in his coach," Lord Welsford whispered to her in return. "We will see you at home, my darling daughter."

Lillian nodded gratefully.

"Thank you, Father."

As she watched Lord and Lady Welsford, along with Timothy, walk to their coach, the intoxicating scent of the Duke drew nearer.

"Good morrow, Your Grace."

"A good morrow to you as well, Lady Lillian. My sincerest apologies for not attending Service with you and your family. I had an important matter which I had to attend to."

"I hope that everything is well."

The Duke nodded.

"Indeed. There is nothing to fret over."

As the Colborne coach slowly went past, Lillian gave a small wave to her mother and father inside.

"Did you not wish to ride with your family?" the Duke inquired.

"Are you not also part of the family, Your Grace?"

The Duke chuckled.

"Indeed. Shall we?"

Lillian followed the Duke to his coach, and they climbed inside. She welcomed the warmth inside the coach with a happy sigh and slid her hands from her fur muff.

"I must admit, I was rather distracted during Service because of your absence."

"I am here now."

"Indeed, you are."

The Duke cleared his throat and sat closer to her.

"There is something I wish to discuss with you."

"What is the matter? Did something happen?"

The Duke chuckled in amusement.

"Nothing is the matter. I apologize for causing you to worry."

"What do you wish to discuss with me?"

"After Lord Bertram caused damage to my study, I was assisting Mrs. Hall and the maids to put things in order, including reorganizing my desk. Inside a compartment in one of the drawers, I found something rather valuable. It was a gift from my mother many years ago, and frankly, I had forgotten it was there. It has been in my family for several generations, and I had been keeping it safe until the time was right."

Lillian sat quietly in the moving coach, waiting for the Duke to continue. He retrieved a small velvet pouch from his breast pocket and slowly opened it, then reached inside to retrieve whatever it contained.

"This ring was my mother's," he announced, uncurling his fingers to reveal it.

Lillian gasped at the sheer beauty of the ring, the ruby sparkling in the light which shone through the window.

"It is exquisite."

"An exquisite ring for an exquisite young woman."

Lillian's brows shot up, and her jaw dropped in disbelief.

"You wish to give that to me?"

"There is no person I would rather give this to than you."

"Are you certain?"

Lillian's heart raced as the Duke took her hand in his and gazed into her eyes.

"I have never been as certain of anything before in my entire life. I love you, Lillian, and I wish to spend the rest of my life with you, if you will have me."

Lillian pursed her lips, and her eyes filled with tears of joy.

"Your Grace..."

"Samuel, if you please."

"Samuel," Lillian tested his name for the very first time, and it was the most natural thing in the world. "Are you asking me to marry you?"

"Indeed I am. Will you make me the happiest man in the world and be my wife?"

"Nothing would make me happier, Samuel."

The Duke's smile broadened, and his eyes flickered with pure joy. Still holding her hand, he slipped the ruby ring onto her finger and leaned closer to her.

Her heart pounded in her chest as their lips touched in a tender moment which was truly magnificent. She had dreamed of that moment ever since she'd first met the Duke, not even knowing who he was. Even then, she'd been unable to rid the memory of him from her mind. Lillian could not believe that she was so lucky as to have such a kind and wonderful man in her life, a man who would soon be her husband.

As they arrived at Welsford House, they joined Lillian's family in the dining room, where a delightful Christmas dinner awaited. In the center of the table was the head of a pig, turkey, vegetables, and rich potatoes. The dessert table was laden with plum pudding, marchpane, and gingerbread, and the aromas of the different foods were alluring.

As the family sat around the table, Lord Welsford rose to his feet and smiled happily at his family.

"As I gaze around me, I consider myself a very fortunate man, as I have all of my loved ones at the table to celebrate Christmas. It is a time for family, for spending time together, and for enjoying the company of the people closest to me. The people I see before me at this moment mean the world to me, and without them, I am nothing. I also wish to welcome His Grace to the table and the family. It is an honor to have you with us this day."

"Thank you, my Lord," the Duke said gratefully, and rose to his feet since he was expected to say a few words as well. "I wish to thank Lord and Lady Welsford for being the most gracious hosts and allowing me to be a part of this wonderful celebration. It means the world to me that I can sit at this table and spend this Christmas with you. I truly am grateful for your hospitality, despite our differences at the start of my visit here."

"Let us not allow the past to place a damper on our celebration, Your Grace," Lord Welsford grinned. "It is a privilege to have you at our table, especially given the recent events of your courtship to Lillian."

"Indeed, and what a delightful courtship it has been thus far."

"You speak of it as though it has been weeks and months, Your Grace," Lillian chuckled.

"With you, forever would not be long enough, my dearest."

Lillian rested her hands on her lap, and a smile appeared on her lips as she gazed at the man she loved.

"I have one last announcement I wish to make before we enjoy this delightful meal," the Duke said and gazed at Lillian. "After the untimely death of my father, followed by my mother's passing, I felt utterly alone in a world that was uncaring and relentless. Life continued, but it felt as though I stood still, unable to move lest I shatter everything around me. And although I was surrounded by people, I felt truly alone. I felt out of place as if I did not have a place in the world. I kept to myself, as I was convinced it was safer. Then, I traveled to London, and things changed. First for the worst, and later for the better. I have found a place in this world, and the perfect person who I wish to stand beside me in that world. Which is why I would like to announce that the lovely Lady Lillian -

"Just Lillian, please," Lillian politely interrupted.

"My sincerest apologies," the Duke chuckled and nodded knowingly. "The lovely Lillian has agreed to marry me."

Lillian giggled as her entire family gasped, and she held her left hand up for all to see.

"To mark the occasion, His Grace has given me this ring, which is a family heirloom."

"What lovely news!" Lord Welsford exclaimed.

"How wonderful," Lady Welsford beamed.

"I believe that congratulations are in order, Yarmouth and sister."

"Thank you," the Duke and Lillian answered at the same time, and that caused them to chuckle in amusement.

"You are already speaking in unison. It is certainly a perfect match if ever I saw one."

"Indeed. And those are so very rare," Lady Welsford smiled at Lord Welsford.

Lord Welsford squeezed his wife's hand, and Lady Welsford turned to Lillian.

"I could not be prouder, my dearest daughter," Lady Welsford beamed at Lillian. "You have found your love match, just as I have, and I am truly delighted for you."

"Thank you, Mother."

It warmed Lillian's heart that her mother was happy for her and, of course, proud that she had found a good man. A better man Lillian would never find, she knew. She was also proud of the Duke, as he seemed to flourish as a member of their family. Not only had he been able to restore his reputation after the scandalous things that Lord Bertram had written about him, but he had found true happiness with Lillian and a family who made him feel at home, for the first time in a long while.

And that was all she ever wanted for him. To be happy, and now, for him to be happy with her.

It was certainly a Christmas that the entire family would never forget.

I AM so glad they were able to be together. Lillian's mother was certainly difficult to please, but she wanted the best for her daughter!

PLEASE CHECK out another Christmas book that I love!

MY DEAR READER

Thank you for reading and supporting my books! I hope this story brought you some escape from the real world into the always captivating Regency world. A good story, especially one with a happy ending, just brightens your day and makes you feel good! If you enjoyed the book, would you leave a review on Amazon? Reviews are always appreciated.

Below is a complete list of all my books! Why not click and see if one of them can keep you entertained for a few hours?

The Duke's Daughters Series
The Duke's Daughters: A Sweet Regency Romance Boxset
A Rogue for a Lady
My Restless Earl
Rescued by an Earl
In the Arms of an Earl
The Reluctant Marquess (Prequel)

A Smithfield Market Regency Romance
The Smithfield Market Romances: A Sweet Regency Romance Boxset
The Rogue's Flower

Saved by the Scoundrel
Mending the Duke
The Baron's Malady

The Returned Lords of Grosvenor Square
The Returned Lords of Grosvenor Square: A Regency Romance Boxset
The Waiting Bride
The Long Return
The Duke's Saving Grace
A New Home for the Duke

The Spinsters Guild
The Spinsters Guild: A Sweet Regency Romance Boxset
A New Beginning
The Disgraced Bride
A Gentleman's Revenge
A Foolish Wager
A Lord Undone

Convenient Arrangements
Convenient Arrangements: A Regency Romance Collection
A Broken Betrothal
In Search of Love
Wed in Disgrace
Betrayal and Lies
A Past to Forget
Engaged to a Friend

Landon House

Landon House: A Regency Romance Boxset
Mistaken for a Rake
A Selfish Heart
A Love Unbroken
A Christmas Match
A Most Suitable Bride
An Expectation of Love

Second Chance Regency Romance
Second Chance Regency Romance Boxset
Loving the Scarred Soldier
Second Chance for Love
A Family of her Own
A Spinster No More

Soldiers and Sweethearts
Soldiers and Sweethearts Boxset
To Trust a Viscount
Whispers of the Heart
Dare to Love a Marquess
Healing the Earl
A Lady's Brave Heart

Ladies on their Own: Governesses and Companions
Ladies on their Own Boxset
More Than a Companion
The Hidden Governess
The Companion and the Earl
More than a Governess
Protected by the Companion

Lost Fortunes, Found Love
Lost Fortunes, Found Love Boxset
A Viscount's Stolen Fortune
For Richer, For Poorer
Her Heart's Choice
A Dreadful Secret
Their Forgotten Love
His Convenient Match

Only for Love
The Heart of a Gentleman
A Lord or a Liar
The Earl's Unspoken Love
The Viscount's Unlikely Ally
The Highwayman's Hidden Heart
Miss Millington's Unexpected Suitor

Waltzing with Wallflowers
The Wallflower's Unseen Charm
The Wallflower's Midnight Waltz
Wallflower Whispers
The Ungainly Wallflower
The Determined Wallflower
The Wallflower's Secret (Revenge of the Wallflowers series)
The Wallflower's Choice

Whispers of the Ton
The Truth about the Earl
The Truth about the Rogue

Christmas Stories
Love and Christmas Wishes: Three Regency Romance Novellas
A Family for Christmas
Mistletoe Magic: A Regency Romance
Heart, Homes & Holidays: A Sweet Romance Anthology

Christmas in London
The Uncatchable Earl
The Undesirable Duke

Christmas Kisses Series
Christmas Kisses Box Set
The Lady's Christmas Kiss
The Viscount's Christmas Queen
Her Christmas Duke

Happy Reading!
    All my love,
    Rose

A SNEAK PEEK OF A LADY'S CHRISTMAS KISS

PROLOGUE

"I have wonderful news!"

Rebecca looked up at her mother, but then immediately turned her head away. Lady Wilbram often came with news and, much of the time, it was nothing more than idle gossip; something that Rebecca herself did not enjoy listening to.

"Yes, Mama?" She did not so much as even look up from her embroidery, but rather continued to sew. The long, bleak winter stretched out before her, dreary and dismal – much like the state of her heart at present – and with very little to cheer her. Her father, the Earl of Wilbram, had made it clear that he was not to go to London for the little Season and thus, Rebecca was to be stuck at home, having only her mother for company. No doubt there would be a great deal more of this sort of occurrence, whereby her mother would burst into the room, expressing great delight at some news or other and, in doing so, remind Rebecca of just how far away she was from it all.

Although I am not certain that I wish to return to London at present. There is the chance that he would be there and I do not think I could bear to see him.

"Rebecca. You are not as much as even listening to me!"

Out of the corner of her eye, Rebecca caught how her mother threw up her hands, but merely smiled quietly. "I am paying you a *great* deal of attention, Mother," she answered, silently thinking to herself that it was the only thing she *could* do, given just how determined her mother was. Having been quite contented with her own thoughts, it was a little frustrating to have been interrupted so.

"You shall soon drop your embroidery once you realize what it is I have to tell you." The promise in her mother's voice was one that finally caught Rebecca's interest, but telling herself not to be foolish, she threw only a quick smile in her mother's direction.

"Yes, I am sure I shall," she promised softly. "Please, tell me what it is. I am almost beside myself with anticipation." Her sarcasm obviously laid heavy on her mother's shoulders, for she immediately threw up her hands in clear disgust.

"Well, if you must behave so, then I shall not tell you the contents of this letter. You shall not know of it! And *I* shall be the one to go to the Duke's Christmas... affair."

Rebecca blinked, her gaze still fixed down upon her embroidery, but her hand stilling on the needle. Had she heard her mother correctly? Had she, in fact, said the words Duke and Christmas? Her stomach tightened perceptively, and she looked up, her irritation suddenly forgotten.

"N*ow* I have your attention."

Her mother's eyebrows lifted and Rebecca set her embroidery down completely, her hands going to her lap. "Yes, Mama, now you have my attention," This was said rather quickly and with a slight flippancy, which Rebecca was certain her mother would hear in her voice, but she did not seem to respond. Seeing her mother's shoulders drop after a moment, her hands going to her sides again, Rebecca let out a slow breath. Evidently, she was forgiven already.

"Yes, I did say the Duke – the Duke of Meyrick, in fact – and I *did* say Christmas."

"What is it he has invited us to?"

"A Christmas house party. It is a little unusual, for it appears to be longer than many others would be. But then again, I suppose as the Duke of Meyrick, he is quite able to do as he pleases!"

"How wonderful!" In an instant, the grey winter seemed to fade from her eyes, no longer held out before her as the only path she had to take. Instead, she had an opportunity for happiness, enjoyment, laughter and smiles – as well as the fact that there would be very little chance of being in company with *him*. No doubt he was either back at his estate or would return to London for the little Season.

"We shall have to speak to your father, of course."

At this, Rebecca's heart plunged to the ground, splintering as it fell. Her father had only just declared that he would remain at his estate over the winter. Even if there *was* an invitation to a most prestigious house party, the chances of him agreeing to attend were very small indeed. Scowling up at her mother, she turned her head away. Why had she told her something such as this only for it to be snatched away again?

"Even if your father should not wish to attend, there is no reason you and I cannot both go," her mother continued immediately, turning Rebecca's scowl into a smile of delight. "He will understand – and given that his estate is not very far from our own, the journey will not be a difficult one. Besides which, it is an excellent occasion for you to make further acquaintances in preparation for the summer season... that is, unless you have any desire to find a gentleman suitor this Christmas."

Rebecca laughed, shaking her head at her mother's twinkling eyes and forcing herself not to think of *him*. Given that her mother and father knew nothing about the affair and, therefore, the abrupt ending to what had taken place, she did not think it wise to inform them of it. "Mama, I am very glad indeed we have been invited. I go with no expectation, just as you ought to do."

Lady Wilbram smiled warmly. "You are quite correct. Now we must make preparations to attend this house party. You will need to look through your gowns and decide which of them is the most suitable. We have time to purchase one or two new gowns also, for there is certain to be at least one Christmas ball! You must be prepared for every possible occasion." Making her way back towards the door with purposeful steps, as though she intended to begin such preparations immediately, Lady Wilbram threw a glance back at Rebecca. Understanding that she was meant to go after her mother, Rebecca set her embroidery down and followed immediately, her heart light and filled with hope.

"Prepared for every occasion, Mama?" she asked as her mother nodded firmly. "What exactly is it that I ought to expect from such a house party? I have only been to one before and it lasted only three days. There was very little that could be done by way of occasion."

"You will find the Duke's house parties are very different experiences," her mother told her, grasping her hand warmly as they walked through the door. "You must have every expectation and, at the same time, no expectation. That is why we must be prepared for every eventuality, making certain that you have an outfit suitable for whatever it is the Duke might decide to do. Christmas is such a wonderful season, is it not?"

Rebecca laughed softly at her mother's excited expression and the delight in her voice. "Made all the more wonderful by this house party," she agreed, wondering how she was going to contain her anticipation for the few weeks before the house party began. "I am looking forward to it. It seems as though winter will not be so mediocre after all."

CHAPTER ONE

After being introduced to everyone, Rebecca took her seat beside her very dear friend, Miss Augusta Moir, whom she was very glad to see. They had exchanged letters quite frequently, and when news of the house party reached Rebecca, one of the first things she did had been to write to Augusta. How glad she was to receive Augusta's letter back, and how delighted to know that she would also be present!

"And that is almost all of us!" Lady Meyrick put her hands out wide, welcoming them all. "There are only one or two other guests still to arrive. I do not know why they have been delayed, but that does not mean we cannot continue. We will soon begin our festivities and they will join us when they are able. Pray, enjoy your conversations for a few minutes longer and, thereafter, the first of our games will begin!"

Rebecca glanced around the room, looking at each and every face and recognizing only a few of them. She did not know exactly who else would arrive, but the company here seemed to be quite delightful. In addition to the fact that she had her dear friend Augusta present also, she was quite convinced it would be an excellent few weeks.

"I do wonder what such festivities will be," Speaking in a hushed whisper, Miss Moir leaned towards Rebecca. "I have heard the Duke is something of an extravagant fellow. Perhaps that will mean this holiday house party will be an exceptional one."

"Yes, but *all* Dukes are known to be extravagant fellows," Rebecca reminded her friend, chuckling. "I would expect nothing less. Although," she continued. "I do wonder where the Duke himself is."

"Did you not greet him when you arrived? He was waiting on the steps to make certain that we were greeted. I certainly was made to feel very welcome by his mother!"

"Yes, he did do so." Remembering the slightly pinched expression on the Duke's face when he had greeted both her and her mother, Rebecca allowed her own concern to remain. "He did not appear to be very glad to see us, however. I will say that for him."

Her friend nodded slowly, her gaze drifting around the room as murmurs of conversation continued between the other guests. "He did not smile once, and certainly I found him rather stiff. His mother, on the other hand, was quite the opposite."

"Mayhap he simply does not like the cold, and given the Season, it is rather cold."

Her friend nodded in agreement, although Rebecca did not miss the twinkle in her friend's eyes. "It is almost as though he does not realize it is wintertime," she remarked, making Rebecca laugh. Her laughter changed into a sigh. "Perhaps he is as I am, in waiting and hoping for the summer to return," Her mind grew suddenly heavy, and she looked away. "I confess I struggle with this long winter. My mood is much improved now that my father has permitted me to come to this house party, however."

Miss Moir laughed softly. "And I am also grateful for your presence here. I am, as you know, a little shy, and I confess that not knowing a great many people here as yet has allowed my anxiety to rise a little."

"You have no need to be at all anxious," Rebecca replied firmly. "You are more than handsome, come from an excellent family and you are well able to have many a conversation with both gentlemen and ladies." She lifted one eyebrow. "At times, I think you pretend this anxiety is a part of your character, for I do not think I would be aware of it otherwise."

"I swear to you, I do not pretend!" Miss Moir exclaimed, only to let out a chuckle and to shake her head, realizing that Rebecca was teasing her. "Do you hope to meet anyone of interest here? Or shall you only be interested in furthering your acquaintances? Christmas is a time where many a gentleman will seek to steal a kiss!"

Hesitating, Rebecca wondered how she was to answer. Her friend was entirely unaware of how her heart had been broken this last Season. Indeed, neither her mother nor her father was aware of it either, but she had borne this heavy weight for many months. The pain lingered still, and there was only one gentleman that she was to blame for it. Her mother and her friends might be hopeful that she would acquaint herself with a gentleman of note with the hope that perhaps the match would be made in the summer Season, but for the present, Rebecca was quite contented to have only acquaintances – and nothing more. Her heart was still too damaged. It certainly had not been healed enough for her to even *think* about becoming closely acquainted with another gentleman.

"Lady Rebecca?"

Rebecca blinked quickly, and then silently demanded that she smile in response. "Forgive me, I became a little lost in thought." Shrugging, she looked away. "I think I should be glad of new acquaintances for the present at least. I do not want nor require anything else."

"I quite understand," Miss Moir looked away, just as Rebecca turned her gaze back towards her friend. Rebecca chose to say nothing further, waiting until her friend looked back at her before she continued the conversation.

"What do you think shall be our first game?" With a quick breath, she returned their topic of conversation to the house party itself. She did not want to go into any particular details about what had happened the previous season, given that a good deal of it was still a secret.

Miss Moir clapped her hands lightly. "I do hope it will be something that will make us all laugh and smile so that there is no awkwardness between any of us any longer." Excitement shone in her eyes, and Rebecca could not help but smile.

"Perhaps there will be some Christmas games! Out of all the ones you can think of, which one would be your favorite?"

The two considered this for some minutes and, thereafter, fell into a deep discussion about whether the Twelfth Night cake or Snapdragon was the very best game. But eventually, their conversation was cut short by Lady Meyrick speaking again.

"I do not think we shall wait any longer. Instead, we shall proceed to the library – but not to dance or any such thing! No indeed, there shall be *many* a game at this house party! Yes, we are to be provided with a great deal of entertainment during your time here, but on occasion we shall be required to make our own entertainment... as we shall do this evening."

Chuckling good naturedly, Rebecca grinned as Miss Moir looped her arm through hers so they might walk together. It appeared this was to be the beginning of a most excellent holiday.

"Do you know who it is that is yet to arrive?" Rebecca asked quietly, as Lady Meyrick spoke quietly to her son, who had interrupted her for some reason.

"No, I do not know," Miss Moir shot her a glance. "But I, myself, would not *dare* to be tardy to something such as this, not when the Duke and his mother have shown such generosity!"

Rebecca shrugged. "Mayhap those still absent are well known to the Duke and had always stated they would be tardy?"

"Mayhap," Miss Moir looked around the room at each guest in turn as they waited to make their way to the library. "I admit I am eager to know who else is to arrive!"

"As am I." Rebecca grinned at her friend just as Lady Meyrick clapped her hands brightly, catching everyone's attention again. The bright smile on the lady's face reflected the joy and anticipation in Rebecca's heart as she waited to hear what it was they were to do.

"We shall begin by playing ourselves a few hands of cards. However, it shall be a little different, for there will be forfeits for those who lose, but gifts for the winner!"

This was met by murmurs of excitement as Rebecca's heart skipped a beat in a thrill of anticipation. She was already looking forward to the game, wondering whether she would have any chance of winning, and if she did, what the gift she would receive might be. A million ideas went through her mind as she battled to catch her breath. There was often a good deal less consideration to propriety and society's customs at such occasions, according to her mother. They were a good deal freer, no longer bound by a set of strict and rigid rules. This was a chance to laugh, to make merry and to enjoy every moment of being here. She was already looking forward to it.

"If you would like to make your way through to the library, the card tables have already been set out."

Unwilling to show any great eagerness for fear of being teased about it by either her mother or her friend, Rebecca stood quietly but did not move.

"Come!" Miss Moir immediately moved forward, tugging Rebecca along with her. "What do you suppose the forfeits might be?"

Rebecca laughed as they made to quit of the room. "I confess I can think of a great many things, but I cannot be certain whether I am correct!"

Miss Moir bit her lip. "I do hope I shall not fail. I would be most embarrassed should I make a fool of myself."

Rebecca pressed her friend's hand. "I do not think you need to have any fear in that regard, my dear friend. The forfeits will not be severe. They may make us a little embarrassed, but it is all in good humor. At least, that is what my mother has told me!"

At this, Miss Moir let out a long breath. "I understand. There will be nothing of any severity."

"Nothing." Rebecca smiled as she walked into the library. "Absolutely. In fact, I do believe there will be nothing in all the time we reside here that should bring you any shame, embarrassment, upset, or anger."

With a smile still upon her face, she walked directly into the room, only to come to a sudden halt. To her utter horror, she perceived a gentleman standing directly opposite her, a gentleman whom she recognized immediately but whom she had vowed never to see again. Her breath hitched as she looked directly at him.

Surely it could not be. Fate would not be so cruel to demand this of her, would not take such a happy occasion and quite ruin it by his presence, would it? And yet, it appeared she was to have such misfortune, for the one gentleman sitting there was the one who had broken her heart. The gentleman who had taken all from her, who had left her with nothing – and at the end, begged her to keep it from the ears and eyes of the *ton*. A gentleman who now went pale as he realized who she was, a shadow in his eyes as he looked at her.

And everything suddenly went very cold indeed.

Oh, no! It seems someone from her past was invited to the house party...someone she didn't want to see again! Check out the rest of the story in the Kindle store The Lady's Christmas Kiss

JOIN MY MAILING LIST

Sign up for my newsletter to stay up to date on new releases, contests, giveaways, freebies, and deals!

Free book with signup!

Monthly Facebook Giveaways! Books and Amazon gift cards!
Join me on Facebook: https://www.facebook.com/rosepearsonauthor

Website: www.RosePearsonAuthor.com

Follow me on Goodreads: Author Page